The cost of doing business : a

P9-AFY-839

F Tarlto

7016520

Tarlton, John S.,

THE COST OF DOING BUSINESS

Also by John S. Tarlton
A Window Facing West

THE COST
OF DOING
BUSINESS

A Novel

JOHN S. TARLTON

BRIDGE WORKS PUBLISHING
Bridgehampton, New York

Published in the United States by Bridge Works Publishing Company, Bridgehampton, New York, a member of the Rowman & Littlefield Publishing Group.

Distributed in the United States by National Book Network, Lanham, Maryland. For descriptions of this and other Bridge Works books, visit the National Book Network website at www.nbnbooks.com

FIRST EDITION

The characters and events in this book are fictitious. Any similarity to actual persons, living or dead, is coincidental and not intended by the author.

Library of Congress Cataloging-in-Publication Data

Tarlton, John S., 1950-
    The cost of doing business : a novel / John S. Tarlton.
      p. cm.
    ISBN 1-882593-42-1 (alk. paper)
    1. Petroleum industry and trade—Fiction.   2. Women oil industry workers—Fiction.   3. Mothers and sons—Fiction.   4. Divorced mothers—Fiction.   5. Grandfathers—Fiction.   6. Louisiana—Fiction.   I. Title.

PS3570.A633 C67 2001
813'.54—dc21

                                        2001035626

10 9 8 7 6 5 4 3 2 1

This one is for my father,
John Stewart Tarlton.

The author wishes to thank Nancy Von Brock, Barbara A. Phillips and Robbye Duke Kees—fine women all. Also, special thanks to Thomas A. Butler for helping to provide food for the table during the composition of this work.

Go in thy native innocence; rely
On what thou hast of virtue; summon all;
For God towards thee hath done his part; do thine.

Paradise Lost: Book IX
John Milton

And there is no trade or employment but the
young man following it may become a hero.

Leaves of Grass
Walt Whitman

PART I

Monday

one

The yellow cur snaps to attention, roused by my sudden and reckless violation of his sacred space. Like a hellhound, his eyes are red and flaring; from his smoking muzzle drips a looping ribbon of viscous drool. He flaunts his terrible teeth.

"Easy, fella, easy, easy," I say, resisting the urge to turn and run for my life. "Let's not get stupid."

Perhaps sensing a bloodbath, the strutting red rooster abandons its mindless dirt pecking and implodes into the darkness beneath the farmhouse steps. A calico cat scoots behind a live oak. An eerie silence descends: Friendly stranger greets surly yard dog in rural tableau.

"Easy, easy," I repeat. "Nice doggy."

Trapped in the open like this, my options are limited. I can try to creep back to the safety of the car or cry for help or hope to use my shoulder bag as a shield should the animal attack. Either that or remain motionless and see what follows—counter the brute's hostile demeanor with unending restraint. That's what I do. For the next three minutes I cease to move, don't even bat a lash. A car passes on the gravel road running before the farmhouse but I am no longer here; I am an appeasing homage newly formed.

"Easy, asshole, easy."

As if rewarding my feigned submission, the yard dog cocks one hind leg high above his yellow back and liberally marks the spot. After first tongue-tasting the steaming puddle, he turns and saunters round the corner of the house, his outsized vanity trailing behind. Non-confrontation is always a vexing letdown to these hotheaded mixed breeds; like much of his species, he boasts a water pipe for a brain.

"Good Rover," I say, letting hold of my breath. "Go find a rabbit to chase."

Thirty miles north of Baton Rouge lies the Parish of Pointe Claire—my present whereabouts on this cloudless December morning. A glimmering shield of white frost blankets the fields and grass pastures along the roadside; a thin layer of brittle ice tops the ditch water. The high levee wall flanking the Mississippi casts its dark specter over the land. My own light-skewed shadow pitches awkwardly across the dirt yard to the foot of the wooden porch steps. The sun shines brightly but without heat. Not a merry soul in sight.

I've driven to Pointe Claire this sky-blue morning to see a man about his property, to examine and make note of his boundary lines, garner facts. I'm trying to solve a puzzle, hoping to draw conclusions from selected signs. It's part of my job. What's at stake, what all the fuss is about, is money. Great green stacks of it.

Having braved my face-off with the yard dog, I become aware of loud voices issuing from inside the farmhouse—

a structure remarkable only in its ability to withstand a string of haphazard additions. Whole rooms have been cobbled together without regard to roof line or materials. Its windows lack shades or blinds, the surrounding grounds devoid of flowers or greenery, not the first hint of feminine treatment. The place looks like somebody's fishing camp. My lucky day.

In one corner of the yard is piled a confusion of empty beer and soft drink cans; a junked car sits marooned on four cement blocks. Inside the house, the several male voices rise to shouting.

"Says who?"

"Me, that's who."

"You and who else?"

"Who?"

"*Shit.*"

As my arrival has surely been noted, a hasty retreat is out of the question. I cannot afford to appear meek or easily intimidated. First impressions are everything.

"*Shit.*"

My first sense is one of foreboding, as if in the midst of these open fields and brown moo cows I have strayed upon a bedeviled farmhouse rife with contending voices. Few facets of the job are more unsettling than arriving for an appointment in the middle of a family fracas. This bunch sounds as if they're about to come to blows. Anything, for God's sake, anything but that.

Climbing the porch steps, I stand before the unpainted front door and knock twice, to which follows not the slightest response. Save for the ceaseless jabber of a television somewhere inside, there is suddenly no trace of life. My hollow stomach turns over; something like dread colors my emotions. After half a minute, I knock again.

The dented doorknob turns slowly on its wobbled axis and the door opens, allowing a gap between door and out-of-square doorframe. In the narrow opening appears one ogling eyeball. The amber eyeball rolls down to my tightly laced work boots, then slowly up my khaki pants and winter coat to my face, unflinching in its gaze. Feeling the skin crawl up the back of my neck, I realize I've just been mentally undressed. Steady, girl, steady. Adversity is what keeps this job interesting.

Remembering my skirmish with the family pet, I stand motionless in the deep shade of the porch. The creepy eyeball disappears and the door swings open, revealing a young black man dressed in overalls and a green fatigue jacket, and wearing a clear plastic shower cap over a head full of glistening curls. He does not speak.

"Good morning," I say, summoning my resolve. "My name is Diane Morris, with Anoco Oil Company. Here to see Henry Dunn."

The young man at the door stares up at me but makes no effort to reply. He appears somewhat disoriented by my height, as if greeting royalty. Is he mute? Disabled? Deranged?

"Who's that?" asks a voice from inside the farmhouse.

"Oil lady," the young man at the door answers. "Says she wants to see Daddy."

"Let her in, fool."

Mud Lake, the shallow no-man's-land bordering the rear of Henry Dunn's property, is a lake in name only, a forgotten backwater set in a queer and distant land. Fed by winter and spring rains, the water depth might reach four feet, swelling the lake's circumference to thirty acres. By mid-August, the water level drops to a foot or less and its surface area will shrink to the size of a small pond. The lake's sole possessors are the few dozen migratory ducks that winter there each year.

As to the lake's legal ownership, it's doubtful the locals ever had cause to worry about it. The low-lying fields surrounding the fluctuating lake shore have never been fenced or farmed; boundary lines are approximated; traditionally, the lands bordering Mud Lake have been treated as unclaimed, open range. Until now, when the entirety of the land beneath the lake will be affected by the next producing oil well. Now it could be worth a small fortune.

Here's the mystery: Who owns Mud Lake and its bottomlands and in what proportions? Are the calculations for ownership of the land underlying the lake to be made at high water or low water? Which of my three landowners bordering the lake has the best claim? Where are the obstacles I must prepare to face? Will I prevail?

My position with Anoco Oil Company bears the title of landman. The landman represents the company's interest in negotiations with private landowners, most often in realms of lease acquisition and drilling operations. To the engineers and bean counters who run Anoco, I am a necessary evil, an overhead expense they would rather do without. But they cannot. If Anoco hopes to drill oil wells on privately owned lands, someone has to negotiate with the landowners because the landowners want to trade face-to-face with a human being in the privacy of their own homes. They refuse to dicker over the telephone; they won't respond to offers posted through the mail or over the

Internet; they decline to drive to town for an appointment. What Anoco requires is an envoy, a hired gun, someone willing to motor into the countryside and lock horns with the landowners. That's me.

To the landowners, I am two-parts Lady-of-Good-Fortune, one-part leering Shylock. They generally rank me and my kind somewhere below car salesmen but just above lawyers, the latter being untouchables. The landowners are always glad to see me but they never turn their backs. I'm either the best thing that's happened to them lately or a lying bitch; it depends on which landowner you talk to, the last landman with whom they dealt.

Like the exterior of Henry Dunn's farmhouse, the fishing camp motif of the interior is maintained to perfection: bare walls and simple furnishings; a state of cleanliness best described as derelict; from a bare lightbulb suspends an ancient and copiously bespeckled strip of flypaper. My first task becomes how to tactfully avoid taking a seat. Look but don't touch.

In the overheated front room, I meet in turn all three of Dunn's grown sons: Lester, Zach and Eugene. Outwardly grim and standoffish, the two older brothers, Lester and Zach, are thin and fluid of frame with long hair braided into coiling dreadlocks, while the younger one, Eugene, is short and muscled. They all have rich black skin and oval, handsome faces. Each of them greets my extended hand with a limp squeeze.

I've noticed that most country people, black or white, are reluctant to make physical contact with a stranger, as if those of us from the city might be carrying some germ, some dreaded measles capable of wiping out the locals. Shaking hands with a woman only heightens their unease.

Time to get this show on the road.

"Is your father around this morning?" I ask.

"He's in the back," Zach says. "Be out in a minute."

The three Dunn siblings and I stand in collective silence and wait. Try as they might, they cannot avoid staring. Eugene, the one wearing the plastic shower cap over his serpent-like curls, digs out a bent cigarette from his flannel shirt pocket and with much ceremony lights it, using a wooden kitchen match. After extinguishing the flame, he puts the still-smoldering stub in a hip pocket of his overalls. On the television in the adjoining room, the emcee of a morning game show plays affable straight man for his Hollywood celebrities, but no one at the Dunn residence is watching. Today's diversion stands stiffly in the middle of their front room, her mouth anointed with raspberry lip gloss.

Stay calm, take your time. Don't start babbling.

The total weirdness of this situation might have once driven me to a fit of stammering, self-conscious chatter, all in hopes of deflecting attention away from myself. Ten years of working with strangers has taught me otherwise; nowadays I just keep quiet and hold my ground. Breathe. Take it in, let it slowly out. Big smiles and lots of teeth. Likely as not the Dunn brothers are equally dismayed by my presence; at least *I* know the purpose of my visit.

Unfurled across a table against the back wall of the front room is a blue-lined ownership map, depicting what looks to be the elder Dunn's property. If nothing else, it will give the Dunn brothers and me something to talk about. As if bound to a common tether, the four of us move in guarded unison around the map.

"As I explained to your father last night when I called, I'd like to inspect the boundary lines at the rear of your property."

A uniformly sullen and suspect response is almost palpable. I might as well be bringing news of foreclosure. The evil landlord done up in gold-stud earrings and leather shoulder bag. *I'm not the bad guy,* I want to shout out, but cannot.

"What's wrong with them?" Zach says.

"Nothing," I say. "There's nothing wrong with your boundaries. I just want to see how your land borders the lake at the rear of the property."

"Mud Lake," Lester says.

"That's right, Mud Lake," I say. "I'd like to see how much of your property borders the shore of Mud Lake."

The Dunn brothers convene a tight huddle over the open map. It's not every day a giant white woman working for an oil company arrives on their doorstep with questions about property lines, and they don't seem to relish the novelty. Like all landowners, they have more confidence in the sanctity of paper and ink than in anything I have to say. Words, they have come to believe, mean different things to different people, whereas a map is something tangible upon which they can rely. They are wrong, of course, but I must proceed carefully. Keep it simple, keep it calm.

I lean over the table and place my hand flat on the map's blue-lined surface.

"This map here," I say, "it's called a Tobin map. It's only a representation of what your property looks like. It's like a picture or a drawing based on the records in the courthouse."

Lester, the darker tinted of the Dunn brothers, reaches out and puts his right thumb firmly on the map beside my

hand; the contrasting black and white skin tones sugges-
tive of our present divide. My fingernails are bitten and
unpolished, his dirty and cracked. Unwittingly, I withdraw
my hand.

"*Lands of Theogene Dunn,*" Lester reads. "That's our
grandfather. All this land here belongs to us."

"I know the land belongs to you," I say. "What I'm saying
is this map is only a sketch of the physical property. The
person who drew this map never set foot on the land itself.
He drew this map based on the property description found
in the deed in the courthouse."

"Who's he?" Eugene says.

"Who?" I say.

"Who drew the map," Eugene says. "Who's he?"

"I don't know the name of the man who drew the map,"
I say. "It might have been a woman."

"Who's she?" Zach says.

"I don't know," I say, waving my hands. "Look, it doesn't
matter who drew the map."

"Says right here, *Lands of Theogene Dunn,*" Lester says.

It's like bobbing for apples, trying to push a bean with
your nose. I wet my lips and count to three. Easy, girl, easy.
Stay cool. The Dunn siblings stand shoulder to shoulder,
awaiting my reply.

"This land belongs to your family and no one disputes
that," I say slowly. "What I'm telling you is the person who
drew this boundary line from the front of your property
back to Mud Lake never inspected the boundary line itself.
He . . . or she, just drew a line from point A to point B on
a piece of paper."

Zach leans forward across the Tobin map looking into
my eyes. His own eyes are black and hard, his expression
pitiless. I've got better sense than to blink.

"What do you want?" he says, his dreadlocks writhing.

Time to cease this morning's cartography lesson and state my business. Despite all the puffed-up manly tension, it's a relief.

"What I want, gentlemen, is to inspect the boundary lines of your property and see how much of it borders Mud Lake."

"You heard the lady," says the grey-bearded figure standing in the doorway behind us.

Henry Dunn, it appears, is not in the habit of raising his voice when addressing his three grown sons.

"You, Zachary," he says, pointing with his black cane. "Bring the wagon round."

At last, a man I can deal with.

two

In a wooden hay wagon behind an antique tractor, the three Dunn brothers, their lanky, soft-spoken father and I set off in the clear morning light for the distant shore of Mud Lake. With each breath, clouds of white vapor rush from our mouths and nostrils and back over our hunched shoulders. We are all shivering, grinning, glad to be out-of-doors and going about our sober errand. If nothing else, it's gotten us out of the dingy house and away from television.

Henry Dunn stands quietly with both hands resting on his stout black cane. The cane's shiny silver crown is fashioned in the shape of a snake coiled upon itself, poised to strike. Upon his head rests a narrow-brimmed felt hat; his faded denim pants are tucked into a pair of Redwing work boots. The brilliant winter sunshine grants his ebon-colored skin a faint brassy glow, as if he were emitting bright light from within. Dunn looks off toward the wooded lowlands at the rear of the property, an amused expression written on his face. He seems to be both concentrated and yet relaxed, ready for any calamity he might be made to face. An enviable frame of mind.

I know more about Henry Dunn and a couple of his neighbors than any of them might ever suspect. I did not just show up here in Pointe Claire this frosty morning with my purse in my hand. Or empty-headed. I spent much of last week researching land titles in the courthouse records. I took time to visit the State Land Office in Baton Rouge to examine the historical documentation of Mud Lake. I made it my business to call on several of the older residents of Pointe Claire deemed as being in the know—those few characters living in every small community who, for the price of a cup of coffee, can pass on the lowdown, both official and unofficial. While my employment has been traditionally reserved for members of the masculine persuasion, I've learned it's less the gender of the landman than the legwork that counts.

I know, for instance, that Theogene Dunn, Henry's father, was the first black man to own property in this remote corner of Pointe Claire Parish. That he suffered poverty and isolation and the threats of bodily harm at the hands of some of his more bigoted neighbors. That he put down fifty hard-earned silver dollars to purchase his land, and that he acquired the money by thrashing every available field hand in the vicinity who, for a shot at only one of those silver dollars, climbed into a roped-off ring with him. But that only explains how Theogene Dunn obtained the money and not why A. E. Baughman, one of the largest property owners in the entire parish, a feudal baron of sorts, would sell eighty acres of his own rich bottomland to a black sharecropper when he desired neither the money nor the ensuing public outcry. And I believe I know the answer to that as well. Baughman sold the land to Theogene Dunn because it showed the rest of the inhabitants of Pointe Claire that he (Baughman) was king. That he could do whatever he wished, whenever and however it pleased him, and no one in the parish could do or say one thing about it. Baughman is long dead now, but his vast holdings remain under the dominion of his only son, A. E. Baughman Jr.

The five of us standing in the bed of Henry Dunn's hay wagon are rocking along at a merry clip. The bracing, open-air ride in the cold has brought about a tentative fellowship, a sense of shared purpose among strangers. While clearly not one of them, for the present I have ceased to be a threat. To maintain balance, we are all forced to plant our feet and lean back against the wagon's high side rails. My long black hair flies high above my shoulders leaving my ears exposed to the cold; my nose is a narrow chip of ice. The white-frosted fields splinter the bright sunshine into glistening patterns of auroral light; bands of snowy egrets crisscross the sky.

Whatever else happens, this wagon ride across the farm will be hard to forget.

Henry Dunn turns his head from the looming apparition of Mud Lake and looks up into my eyes. His expression is quizzical, almost gleeful.

"This land belonged to my Daddy," he says. "When he passed, it came to me. When it's my time, it goes to my three sons here."

"I understand that, Mr. Dunn. What I'd like to see this morning is how much of your land borders the lake. Are there any markers showing the width of your property along the shoreline?"

"You bet there are," he says, nodding his head. "My Daddy and me marked them ourselves. Put down buggy axles on each line."

"That's good, Mr. Dunn. Very good. Existing boundary markers will be a big help."

Everybody gets a break now and then. This might be mine.

As a younger woman, just getting my start in the oil industry, I was timid and suffered qualms about all landowners. I took pains not to react to their startling outbursts regarding God and family, their heartrending eruptions of grief and suffering, their greed, their desolation. I bent over backwards trying not to appear the fast-talking outsider. Yet often I was left bewildered by some of their more exotic behaviors.

Ten years ago this month, on the third day at my new job with Anoco Oil Company, I was sent to the home of an elderly landowner in Terrebonne Parish who owned one thousand acres of pristine marshland. Anoco wanted to lease all of it. I was given a neat stack of legal documents for the widow to sign, directions to her remote bayou home and sent packing. None of my male co-workers bothered to mention that the old woman was mad. That was all part of getting the new girl's attention, part of the fun.

Assholes.

Mrs. Lebeau was sitting on her cypress porch swing peeling red potatoes when I drove up beneath the oak trees at the front of the house. Before I could state my business, before I could climb the tall front steps, the old woman announced she had spoken just that morning with John F.

Kennedy. That's what she said. She said the ghost of John F. Kennedy appeared at her bedside each morning at dawn and answered all her questions about current events. Mrs. Lebeau was short, with watery blue eyes and a tight grey bun atop her round head; on her feet she wore white rubber ankle boots. When she smiled, the wrinkles in her face ran every which way, like the crooked lines of a parish road map.

Mrs. Lebeau took me by the hand and led me through the rambling house to her sunlit bedroom. The lingering fragrances of clean cotton, spearmint gum and perfumed bath powder reminded me of my own mother's cluttered bedroom; the pungent scent sent me all the way back to my childhood. It was there beside the bed, Mrs. Lebeau said, that Kennedy appeared faithfully each morning. In response to her queries, the slain president tapped out his answers one by one on the headboard—two taps for yes, one for no. The trick, she confided, was in knowing how to phrase the questions. As tribute to my stunned civility, Mrs. Lebeau told me Kennedy had nice hands and was a snappy dresser. Then she laughed and flashed the many wrinkles in her face.

She was somebody's grandmother, I reminded myself. She meant no harm. My objective was to get the papers signed before President Kennedy intervened and stopped Anoco from drilling its oil well.

After heavy November rains, the brown water of Mud Lake has emerged out of its low bottom and run across the flat expanse of an adjoining field where it engulfs a big stand of bald cypress. In the high yellow grass alongside the lake, Henry Dunn orders the hay wagon to a halt.

"They right in here somewhere," he says, gesturing with his black cane. "You boys get down and look smart. Buggy axles is hard to miss."

But miss them we do. Unwilling to sit and watch the men do all the work, I join the Dunn family's frantic search in the tall grass. After an hour all we have for our combined efforts is an acre of beaten-down Johnson grass, a busted shovel handle and muddy boots.

We find a cow skull, a rusty pair of pliers, an empty beer bottle, a fishing pole. But no buggy axles. Unable to keep my big trap shut, I let my mouth overload my better judgment.

"And you're sure, Mr. Dunn, you're sure you and your Daddy placed those buggy axles right along in here somewhere?"

Henry Dunn looks at me but does not bother to reply. Our initial bounty of mutual goodwill appears to be waning. He blinks his ruddy brown eyes and smiles wryly. But I won't leave it alone.

"Do you think someone might have removed those axles, Mr. Dunn? Why would anyone go to that much trouble?"

Eugene, bits of wet Johnson grass sticking to his plastic shower cap, digs out another cigarette from his shirt pocket and lights it with a kitchen match.

"*Shit.*"

three

I didn't so much gain entry into the oil industry as stumble into it. Literally. Ten years ago, at age twenty-three, I contacted Anoco Oil Company about an opening in their sales department. Newly estranged from my husband Ray and with a young son to support, I made up what I lacked in experience with what I possessed in need: I needed a job and I needed it in a hurry. Anoco requested that I appear for an interview at their corporate headquarters on Essen Lane in Baton Rouge. On the appointed date I arrived at Anoco's offices, only to exit the elevator on the wrong floor and wander into the exploration department. There were sixteen men and no women in this division, and every pop-eyed one of them sat there staring. Collecting themselves, they offered me in quick succession a doughnut, coffee or tea, a glass of water, a magazine, a tour of the premises. Two of the young trainees got into a friendly shoving match as to whose chair I was to be offered; from the back of the room came a hooting salute. My new plaid skirt suddenly shrank to the size of a dinner napkin. I felt flattered but too much the center of attention to be at ease. *Down, boys, down.*

Finally, one of the senior managers emerged from his carpeted lair and restored order. Once imposed, this same manager observed there had never been a woman working in the exploration division—an untenable state of inner-office affairs as proclaimed by Anoco's new upper management, an anachronism no longer to be tolerated. I was hired on the spot.

Working in the formerly all-male exploration department took some getting used to, but once the guys accepted that I was not there to take their phone messages, make coffee, have sex with them or wipe their chins, we made progress. The most resistant bloc of new colleagues was the contingent of older men, members of my father's generation. They were all perfectly charming, jovial, conducting themselves as proper Southern gentlemen, but below the surface my hiring served as a kind of irksome tonic; they all lined up and took their medicine but some of them let it be known they didn't have to like it. Their basic contention was that, being a woman, I would pale under the hard knocks of day-to-day negotiations with conservative country types, meaning the menfolk; that while I was a fast learner and a good sport, I was out of my league. Nothing personal, they said, but it all boiled down to a difference in temperament. Resenting the same tiresome obstacles placed in my path, I went ballistic.

"Assholes," I called them, each and every one. But it didn't stop there.

Brashly, I assured the naysayers that I had no intention of trying to conduct myself *like a man.* For better or worse, I told them, I planned on bringing to the job everything I possessed, body and mind. While gaining their undivided attention, I failed to win over all my new co-workers. There remains to this day a small cell of contrarians who are unable to view me as anything other than a rebellious, overgrown shrew with a burr under her saddle, someone who will one day get her comeuppance. On the up side, three women are now on staff in Anoco's exploration division so the oddity of a female in their midst is something the men have put behind them. Mostly.

The first question many women ask when I describe my job to them is how do I ever decide what to wear. Not what do I like about the oil industry, not how do I like traveling all over the state haggling toe to toe with strangers, but what clothes do I wear. I find the question vaguely insulting, as if to say my vocation were merely a fashion venue, an extended runway strut across south Louisiana. As if I don't get enough attention when I walk into a room the way it is. The choice of work clothes is simple: If I plan to be out crossing fences, walking through fields or pastures examining property lines, I wear boots and pants, a comfortable blouse, possibly a jacket, not much in the way of jewelry. If I'm meeting a consulting attorney for a nice lunch in town, I wear a dress and heels. If impelled, I dress up well.

A quarter mile down the gravel road from Henry Dunn's place sits the home of Amanda Snow, ageless, solitary farmer and local curiosity. I got a full measure of Mrs. Snow's feisty charm when I spoke with her on the telephone last night.

"Mrs. Snow, my name's Diane Morris. I work for Anoco Oil—"

Amanda Snow didn't wait for the close of my greeting. Her laughter had an edge to it.

"I know all about that outfit you work for, honey," she said. "What do you want from me?"

"I'm going to be up in Pointe Claire tomorrow morning, Mrs. Snow, and I'd like to visit with you if I may? I'm meeting with Henry Dunn at nine o'clock, and I could stop by your place around noon. Would that be convenient?"

There followed a short pause filled by the background blare of a television.

"It's that Mud Lake business, isn't it?" she said. "You and that pack of thieves you work for have got your eye on something back there. Everybody in Pointe Claire knows that."

The last thing I needed was another dustup with an irate landowner. Every door I opened revealed a charging bull. Is this my doing? Do I bring this down on myself?

"Yes, Ma'am," I said, trying to keep my voice even, "it's about Mud Lake. I'd like to stop by and ask you some questions if you have no objection."

"Come on if you're coming, honey. I'll either be here or I won't."

Not the most promising of beginnings, but I have long since learned the folly of forecasting the mind-set of a landowner. Stay calm, stay focused, try not to anticipate.

Amanda Snow's prejudicial views aside, Anoco Oil Company has no predetermined interest in how the ownership underlying Mud Lake is resolved. All the landowners bordering the lake leased their mineral rights to Anoco two years ago, so that no matter who owns where and in what proportion, Anoco's interest is established. The local courts may require that Anoco become embroiled in lengthy legal proceedings if all parties claiming ownership to the lowlands around the lake cannot reach an amicable property settlement. Naturally, Anoco, as operator of the producing wells in the area, would prefer a speedy boundary agreement—hence the current assignment dispatching me to Pointe Claire Parish. No pressure, no added stress, just get the job done or else.

Amanda Snow's red brick home sits back off the gravel road beneath a pecan grove. After cruising up the limestone driveway, I park at the open door of the garage behind a canary-yellow station wagon. A reckoning of my appearance in the rearview mirror confirms the open-air ride in Henry Dunn's hay wagon took its toll, though there's no quick fix for excessive height or a too-narrow nose.

"Like making mud pies, we work with what we've got."

Fortunately my fair skin tans easily under the outdoor regimen of my job, so a touch of mascara generally gets me through the day. A quick hair brushing, a dab of lip gloss, and I'm back in business. I take a deep breath and try to clear my mind. Showtime.

After years of seeking the confidence of strangers, I have learned to rid myself of all expectations. Complex strategies or overzealous goals will only hang me up. Persistence, empathy, open-mindedness are my strongest allies. My womanly weapons of choice. The quick-draw temper is my Achilles' heel.

With no visible sign of hostile animals about, I cross Amanda Snow's driveway and head for the front door. In ten years of calling on landowners, I have been attacked by family pets, chased by livestock, beset by yard fowl, pelted with rocks by spirited farm children. I was once run up a hackberry tree by a three-hundred-pound pig named Bruce, a vicious animal who gave up his hot pursuit only after being bribed with a shovel full of lukewarm slop. Prior to my rescue, Bruce's owner managed to get off a snapshot that circulated through Anoco's corporate offices under the accompanying epigraph: "Tall Woman Up A Short Tree".

Reaching Amanda Snow's front door without incident, I knock several times but no one answers. Circling back around to the kitchen door off the garage, I knock again. Nothing happening inside the house but the chronic babble of a television talk show. Another sordid airing of private woe.

"It's not real, people," I grumble, "it's all a pathetic shadow play. Wake up."

Moving to the rear of the house, I turn the corner behind the garage where I come face to face with the barrel of a silver-plated revolver. Standing behind the business end of the pistol is a petite, silver-haired white woman dressed in jeans and a red jacket and muddy rubber boots. Because she is tiny and I am tall, the woman is standing almost under me, the round pistol barrel aimed steadily up at my chin. My feet feel suddenly rootbound; the blood rushes from my head.

"It's me, Mrs. Snow. Diane Morris. With Anoco."

She lowers the pistol to about the level of my waist, but keeps me covered.

"I never shot an Amazon before," she says. "You ought to be more careful, honey. You could get yourself killed."

Which is another way of saying I'm a stranger to these

parts and until notified otherwise, don't start any funny business.

"I knocked at the door, Ma'am. Please put the gun down."

Amanda Snow slips the pistol into the right side pocket of her red jacket and steps carefully back. Though I know her to be in her sixties, she moves like a woman half her age. Her face is tanned and unlined and her grey eyes are shining. I had hoped to parlay our common gender to an advantage. Instead the old bitch pulled a gun on me.

Slow down, stay cool. Make friends and bring her over to my side.

"If you think I've got nothing to do but sit around and wait for your kind to show up," Amanda Snow says, "then you better think again."

Ignore the cheap shot and push on.

"It's a pleasure to meet you, Mrs. Snow. I've heard so many interesting things about you."

Amanda Snow's dry laugh cannot conceal her skepticism.

"Save your breath," she says. "I'm too old for your sly tricks."

"I'm just trying to do my job, Ma'am."

"Well, you're too late," she says, turning and moving toward the garage. "They're already gone. I checked them first thing this morning."

"What's gone, Mrs. Snow?"

Amanda Snow turns back to face me and smiles, enjoying her game of cat-and-mouse.

"Those boundary markers you're so hell-bent to find," she says. "Back there on the shore of Mud Lake."

"Somebody stole your boundary markers?"

"I just told you that, honey. You sound like an echo."

Before I can reply Amanda Snow turns again and heads for the garage. I have to move quickly.

"This is important, Mrs. Snow. If someone has been tampering with the boundary markers along the lake, I need to know about it."

This time her laugh is more like a squawk.

"There's no tampering about it," she says. "Those markers are *gone*. Nothing left but empty holes."

"I'd like to have a look at those holes, Mrs. Snow. That is if you don't mind showing them to me?"

She stops and turns, peering into my face.

"You want to see the holes?" she says, her grey eyes narrowed.

"I've come a long way, Mrs. Snow, with nothing much to show for it."

"Except the holes," Amanda Snow reminds me.

"Yes, Ma'am. Except those damn holes."

It takes Amanda Snow a full thirty seconds to decide if she is going to humor me or not. Without the woman's confidence, I have nothing.

"Suit yourself," Amanda Snow says finally, turning back toward the garage, "but to my way of thinking, once you've seen one hole in the ground, you've seen them all."

Her point is well taken, but I have a job to do.

As the majority of oil and gas exploration takes place outside the confines of cities and towns, my job routinely takes me into the more rural parishes of Louisiana such as Pointe Claire. Though I always correspond with landowners in advance, they are often surprised to discover an unaccompanied woman standing at their door. After elaborate, sometimes awkward introductions—some form of giddy recognition that I am the tallest female ever to grace their threshold—the man of the house and I take our seats at the kitchen table, the obligatory, ground-zero point for all matters pertaining to family business. The wife putters close by, tending to dinner or the remnants of a prior meal or simply cleaning, but mostly listening. The man checks and then rechecks his watch, sips his coffee, fields my queries regarding cattle prices or crop conditions, killing time until my male counterpart finally shows up so we can all get down to the business at hand. I never try to rush things. Sooner or later a light will dawn on Papa-Daddy that the person he is dealing with this morning is already seated at his table.

Often as not, the wife is two or three jumps ahead of her husband and noticeably amused. It's certain she has witnessed ten thousand all-male horse-trading sessions, alternately conducted over kitchen tables or back fences or the hoods of pickup trucks, and she can predict the dreary posturing before it even gets started. But today's negotiations have a slight variation, and she's on to it.

And should she happen to learn that I, too, must organize and run a household and unstop a sink if necessary, all the while holding down a full-time job, her customary reticence can be made to lessen. (I am not above asking for a cake recipe if I think it will tip the scales.) If I can get the wife seated at the kitchen table actively participating in the discussion, I'm halfway home. With the wife at the table, the more terse, inflexible, body-pounding style of negotiating practiced by her husband can be channeled into a spirit of collaboration and mutual gain. Papa-Daddy won't like it, but he'll soon realize he's been isolated and outflanked. Then it's just a matter of time before he becomes impatient, consents to basically whatever his wife and I have agreed upon, and storms off to visit his gloomy cattle.

⚬

Riding beside Amanda Snow in the cab of her farm truck (I feel like a child sitting beside her new doll—only the doll is driving), the two of us journey back across the unplowed fields to the rear of the property. With each dip, rise or drop-off, the truck's overwound suspension throws us high off the bench seat into the air, making it impossible not to laugh. We are two young girls astride an elephant's back. To be heard, Amanda Snow has to raise her voice above the roar of the truck's engine.

"I never knew my mother," she shouts. "She died when I was a baby. That left my father and me. Some folks thought he was a harsh man, but he was just particular. He had a farm to look after, a little girl to raise and only his two hands to do it with. And he didn't suffer fools easily."

"Now it's all yours?" I yell back.

The pickup bounds across the unlevel fields.

"I lived my life on this land," Amanda Snow says. "After my husband was killed, I worked every inch of it myself. I worked the fields, harvested the corn, mended the fences. You ever milked a cow, honey? Slaughtered a hog?"

"I'm a city girl, Mrs. Snow. I buy my milk at the Bet-R-Store."

Amanda Snow shakes her head sadly. My fairy godmother dressed in farm clothes.

"A city girl," she says. "Fiddlesticks."

She guns the engine and throws the truck across a small drainage ditch, tossing us both high off the seat—my head caroms off the cab's ceiling. An assortment of shovels and farm tools clamors in the pickup's metal bed.

"After my husband passed," Amanda Snow says, downshifting into second gear, "I was left all alone. So I built the new brick house and never looked back. What little I can't grow, I get at the grocery. If I need a helping hand, I hire it. God helps those who help themselves, honey."

In the tall grass beside the shore of Mud Lake, Amanda Snow stops the pickup truck and points to the newly dug holes where she and her father buried six-foot iron rods marking the corners of their property.

"You city girls might have another name for them," she says, her grey eyes gleaming, "but around here we call them holes in the ground."

And a court of law might call it destruction of property.

"To the best of your recollection, Mrs. Snow, these holes mark . . . *marked* the corners of your property?"

"It's the iron rods that are missing," she says, "not parts of my brain."

"Now tell me, Mrs. Snow, who do you know would spend the time and energy required to dig up and haul off a bunch of old boundary markers?"

Amanda Snow stares out across the tall grass toward the rippled surface of Mud Lake, then back at me. Her gaze is more tempered than before, as if the bumpy ride across her fertile lands has brought the two of us closer together.

"Honey," she says, "if you haven't figured out the answer to that, you're in worse shape than I thought."

Pointe Claire's missing boundary markers may cast doubt on existing land claims, making my job of concluding a boundary agreement less feasible. I wonder which of my landowners has the most to gain by unclear boundaries. To what lengths is this person planning to disrupt my work? When will I be seen as part of the problem?

four

I take the river road running alongside the Mississippi back to Baton Rouge. The ridge of high pressure that pushed through south Louisiana overnight lowered the temperature and swept the humid haze before it. The wide sky whirls clear and cold above the earth—a profusion of wind, copper sunlight and open spaces. The river road is not the quickest way to town but the winding drive beside the levee is both soothing and engenders thought.

"Let the lazy river flow," I instruct a high-flying egret. The snow-white bird beats a graceful path through the thin air.

I do have a life away from oil. One that is becoming more frantic and increasingly masculine. My father and I never discussed the prospect of living under the same roof; I failed to see it coming. He simply arrived for dinner one Saturday night toward the end of last summer and never got around to leaving.

After moving some of his clothes, a few toiletries, into my spare bedroom, Pop let slip he might stay for a while.

Not an immediate problem as far as I was concerned, though curious; his own comfortable home was located not ten blocks away. Within days he took over preparation of the evening meals and the grocery shopping. He's a better cook than I am, though that admission falls short of flattery; his specialties are fresh seafoods grilled on the pit and then tossed with salads or pasta. He can do extraordinary things with hamburger and skinless chicken meat. While I'm at work, he likes to putter around the yard, keep the grass cut. He picks up Tim, my twelve-year-old son, from school in the afternoon. I never imagined our lives becoming this entwined; at times I wish it wasn't so.

Tim and I had always faced the world together, two hearts, one mind. Within days of Tim's birth, my husband Ray landed a public relations job for a string of gambling casinos along the Gulf, where his fondness for racing and games of chance flourished. Ray began staying away from Baton Rouge for days, sometimes weeks at a stretch. When he was home, he was restless, bored, the freewheeling days of our courtship truncated by a newborn in a baby seat. As always, Ray wanted to move fast, and Tim and I could not keep up. Eventually, he left us behind.

Tim is the big winner in his grandfather's recent change of domicile. Omitting me, their heads are constantly together, convening an ongoing male conspiracy of off-color jokes and sports addiction. Their latest passion is Greek mythology. They spend hours thumbing through reference books exploring the accounts of Olympian gods and goddesses, reading aloud the exploits of Greek heroes, like Theseus and Achilles and the wayward Odysseus. The relationship has provided Tim with the father he's hardly known; it has given my father a piece of his life back. It put me on the sidelines.

What's a daughter to do? My father stands six-feet-six with a personality wanting extra space, room to move and wallow in. He's like a gorilla on good behavior; though friendly, he needs watching. No longer amused by fishing or golf, Pop's province of pet obsessions has narrowed to the particulars of daily life at my house. Funny, but I don't recall ever seeking his opinion. When not preoccupied with Tim and me, he gets waylaid by the future.

Following his retirement from L.S.U. last year, Pop came to the conclusion there was no point in doing anything. His life would run its course and nothing could be done to alter it. He would not make plans, would not so much as buy a new fishing lure for his unused tackle box. Why bother? If the tires went flat on the parked boat trailer, so be it. If the golf game he spent his entire adult life perfecting went to ruin overnight, then good riddance. What was the point? Instead he sat around watching cable television day and night or spent hours peeking out the kitchen window as if some dark apparition were about to materialize. It's like he was already living a kind of self-imposed, limbo death. A glum warm-up for the real thing.

I tell him it's not healthy for a man to spend all his time hanging around the house, brooding, playing games with a twelve-year-old. I encourage him to get out, play golf, take a trip, do something, *anything*, but Pop has a knack for suddenly growing obtuse and hard of hearing, staring into space. He seems perfectly content to park himself at my kitchen table and drink coffee, cavort, advise, pontificate. He's worked himself into the thick of things, and Tim's the apple of his eye. My possible inconvenience be damned.

"Now let me get this straight," Pop said, clearing a space at the breakfast table this morning. "After his gift of fire to the men, Prometheus has them butcher an ox and divide the meat into two piles. Is that right?"

"Two *heaps*," Tim said, reading from a picture anthology of Greek myths.

"Two heaps it is," Pop said, placing a fork and a spoon side by side. "Prometheus tells the men to put the hams and roasts in this heap, the scraps and guts in the other. Like so?"

"Like so," Tim said.

My twelve-year-old son is at an age when learning can be made an enticing sport. His grandfather has the flair for keeping him in a state of near revelry.

"It's late, Tim," I said. "Finish your cereal."

"Prometheus then tells the men to hide the heap of meat beneath skin and bones, and to cover the guts with slabs of shining fat," Pop said. "Is that right?"

"Skin and bones, slabs of snow-white fat," Tim said.

Like his grandfather, Tim is going to be tall and strong of stature. I love him so much I sometimes worry how he exists when I'm not around. What's to keep his heart and lungs, liver and spleen behaving as they should? What might happen to him if I were not there to protect him? Would the world cease turning over the demise of one twelve-year-old boy? Or would only mine?

"So then Prometheus invites Zeus to pick the heap he wants the men to burn in his honor, only Zeus chooses the heap of guts," Pop said.

"Prometheus tricked him," Tim said, grinning. "He tricked old Zeus."

"And for *that*," Pop said, "Zeus sent down to earth the beautiful Pandora."

"Look, guys," I interrupted, "after I drop Tim off at school, I've got to drive to Pointe Claire. Let's move it."

Avoiding eye contact, Pop and Tim tried to act as if that were their first encounter with the story of Pandora. They both know they can always count on a swift reaction from me should their heckling wander too far afield.

"The story is right here in the book, Mom," Tim said. "Tell her about the miseries."

"Now it was Pandora," Pop said, "who opened the forbidden jar and set loose the miseries: Greed, Gossip, Envy, Despair, Old Age, Deceit."

"*Eat!*"

Tim and Pop sat motionless, thick as thieves, munching cereal, unfazed by my outburst. All smug and incorrigible grins.

"I think you two have it backwards," I said, taking my bowl to the kitchen sink. "A world of men without women, now that would be misery. I'm leaving."

After my mother died of cancer two years ago, Pop stopped answering the telephone. I would swing by his house on my way home from work and find him sitting in the kitchen with the lights off, unfed, unshaven. His long years of meticulous living unraveling at the edges.

One day I discovered he had enlarged hundreds of old photographs of my mother and affixed them to every wall, bookcase, cabinet door and flat surface in the house, including the bathrooms. The effect was appalling, like walking through a claustrophobic study of one woman, a willful fixation with the dead and departed.

While Pop's general outlook has improved noticeably since moving in with Tim and me, he's still not the same sunny spirit he was once. He remains pensive, vulnerable, moody. Gone is the aura of strength and goodness that seemed to radiate from him when friends or former students stopped him on the city streets and sought his favor, plumbed his mind. He always had a knack for bestowing his fair counsel as a tree bears fruit without guile or intent. Rarely a month goes by that someone doesn't tell me how Pop changed her life.

These days he's like the lone survivor of some devastating crash, healed of body, sound of mind, but spiritually wrecked, unprepared for the business of enduring. Perhaps his moving in with Tim and me can be seen as a last-ditch effort to set the world aright before his own leave-taking. But nowhere did I sign on as Daughter of the Decade; I've still got one or two daydreams myself.

"What you need is a companion, Pop," I keep telling him. "Someone you can do things with, go places with."

"That's a piece of advice you might try following yourself," he shoots back.

It's Pop's view that I can have any man I desire. Just snap my fingers and they'll come running. A father's fantasy.

"The big difference between you and me, Pop, is that I'm looking."

"You're too particular," he says, stirring his coffee in slow reflective turns.

"Damn particular," I say. "I'm looking for someone who wants me for what I am. Who's loving and faithful. And he must be tall. No more short men, you hear? No more adulterous short men with their raging lunacy. I want a man who can stand flat-footed and look me in the eye. That's not so much to ask, is it? You run across a tall, loving, reliable man, you point him out to me. I'll take care of the rest."

But here I am preaching to the choir again. Pop disliked Ray from the beginning.

"I told you not to marry him, didn't I?" Pop says, still stirring. "Didn't I tell you he couldn't be trusted? Didn't I try to warn you?"

"Yes, Pop, you spoke, I refused to listen, then things went to hell in a handbasket. Chalk one up for the kindly old sage."

"So you got any prospects?" he says, beating me to the punch.

"Zero," I say, moving to the fridge. "How about yourself? Met any hot numbers in the checkout line?"

"Your mother was the best friend I ever had."

"You don't have to find a substitute for her," I say. "Just keep a lookout for someone you can get along with. Like our neighbor, Mrs. Haygood."

As if stuck with a needle, Pop jumps in his seat.

"Crystal Haygood is suffering from matrimony of the mind," he says, "her sole requirement being the groom be capable of fogging a mirror."

As usual, there's a goodly measure of truth to Pop's pronouncements. Crystal Haygood's search for a soul mate sheds a brazen intensity. Yesterday I was out front admiring Pop's yard work when I caught sight of the woman—dressed for battle in her neon-blue kimono—bearing down on me from next door. The blue kimono, a recent acquisition from her ten-day trip to Japan, is purported to have the power of casting a spell on any unwary male who lays his eyes on it. She's been wearing it ever since her return. So far Pop has resisted its seductive charms.

"Where's that good-looking father of yours?" she said, joining me in the yard. "He's a hard man to pin down."

"He's just naturally shy, Mrs. Haygood. He mentioned your name to me just this morning."

"He did?" she said, brightening. "Well, it goes to show

you. We single girls have to get out now and then just to keep our names in the running. Don't we?"

"Yes, Ma'am."

Crystal Haygood is a widow in her mid-sixties—a long-necked, heavy-breasted, thin-legged woman—and is by every standard healthier and more vigorous than a horse. According to neighborhood legend, her amorous escapades over the past decade would cause a college coed to blush. Her reference to *we single girls* had a meaning all its own. It was a candid allusion to the fact that I am thirty-three-years old and divorced, and her son Peter is still available for the taking.

"Are you seeing anyone?" she said.

"No, Ma'am."

Her son Peter owns the Haygood Carpet Center in Baton Rouge and sells bundles and bundles of inexpensive carpet to poor people. His garish mug can be seen hawking his wares day and night on every television channel. The louder he talks, the more you save. Last year, at the behest of his mother, Peter and I went out together on several occasions, dinner, a couple of movies. Unfortunately Peter is dumb as a donkey and either endures a congenital hip disorder or spent the entirety of three evenings in my company sporting a gigantic erection. I could have hung a fern from it.

Peter wasted no time letting me know that my height was no problem for *him*.

"Let them stare," he told me, his pants bulging. "If they don't have anything else to do, let them stare."

I blame no one but myself. All future dating, I have solemnly sworn, shall include no misfits, small men, or charity cases. Cross my heart and hope to die.

PART II

Tuesday

five

A fter meeting with Henry Dunn and Amanda Snow yesterday morning, I spent the remainder of the day in my office poring over land maps and title deeds, trying to reduce the issue of ownership under Mud Lake to its narrowest terms. Experience tells me the more elegant the design of the proposed boundary settlement, the greater likelihood all concerned parties will agree to it. The crux of the proposal rests on my premise that ownership to the lake bottom be determined at high water. That way it's only a matter of projecting assumed property lines along the shore of Mud Lake.

Mud Lake at High Water

Lands of A. E. Baughman Jr.

Lands of Henry Dunn

Lands of Amanda Snow

See how simple it is? By projecting assumed boundary lines into the center of Mud Lake at high water, I arrive at each landowner's proportionate share of the lake bottom. It's easy, coherent and impartial. What could be better than that?

Is this then the motive behind the disappearing Pointe Claire boundary markers? Does someone believe obscure property lines will impede a settlement? Where's the advantage in delay? If none of the landowners bordering Mud Lake can prove their boundary lines, how will I turn the deal?

Presently I am north of Baton Rouge, on my way to Pointe Claire Parish again. Though the temperature has climbed into the upper forties this morning, the sky arches high and wide, deflecting rays of sunlight along the cold curve of the earth. Above the huge cane field on my left, long bands of cattle egrets flap their way toward the blue horizon. To my right, the great humpbacked levee holds the sweeping Mississippi at bay.

With no hay wagon rides featured on today's schedule, I settled on a dark grey corduroy skirt and matching jacket, a white turtleneck sweater and black loafers. Warm and comfortable, yet dressy. One day a week or so in boots is enough.

A. E. Baughman Jr. is no stranger to the hardworking men and women at Anoco Oil Company. Anoco has drilled four producing oil wells on Baughman's home place within the last year. As his neighbor Henry Dunn so aptly puts it: *them that got, gits.*

And why, I cannot figure, does this occurrence always come as such a wide-eyed surprise to so many people? If so-and-so owns the majority of land in the Blue Rock Township, guess who has the best chance of having hydrocarbons discovered under his property? It's simply a game of favorable geology and numbers. There is no sleazy conspiracy between oil companies and large landowners to locate oil wells solely beneath the latter's property. On the contrary, the oil companies are often loath to deal with the likes of Baughman because people like him are never satisfied until they have beaten you back into a corner and worked every nuance of the trade in their favor.

Them that got, gits.

My first face-to-face encounter with Baughman took place one blistering morning last summer. The powers at Anoco had placed into my possession a company check made out to Baughman in the amount of one million dollars and some change, representing the first six months' royalty payment from his four producing oil wells. I had never seen so many numerals embossed across the face of a check; while money may not resolve all problems, it does seem to make them more sufferable. Baughman's check, it occurred to me, was a kind of passport, a voucher admitting the bearer into a way of life, a way of seeing and experiencing the world for which few have preparation. The paper itself admitted to a singular quality, as if it were a sliver from Christ's cross. Naturally, I thought it might impress Baughman as well.

I arrived at Baughman's sprawling ranch compound around noon one day in July, the million-dollar check tucked safely in my briefcase. The housekeeper who answered my knock led me through the living room to a sunken den where Baughman lay supine in an oversized recliner, watching television. The air-conditioning system had lowered the room's temperature to the point of freezing; a glass wall of windows dripped with leaden condensation. Without turning his gaze from the giant television screen, he motioned for me to be seated on an antique oak church pew standing to one side. It was standard dismissive procedure practiced by big-time landowners: it meant take a seat, all concerns will be addressed in order of their importance.

By all appearances a late riser, Baughman was still dressed in his cotton pajamas, his big, blotchy bare feet reclined at eye level—all ten toenails were yellow and buckled and encrusted with a flaky green fungus. I've seen livestock with prettier feet; I wanted to gag. On the floor beside the recliner lay a one-eyed German shepherd.

On the obligatory giant television screen, a young married couple was in the midst of revealing to a rapt studio audience the gruesome details of their sex life. The husband, it was admitted, had a fondness for periodically assailing his mate with foreign objects, fruits, vegetables, blunt devices. The wife—an attractive brunette who used her hands freely when she spoke—professed to being no prude and even consented to the occasional use of organic matter but vehemently drew the line at kitchen utensils. The studio audience was bitterly divided.

"What can I do for you, Miss?" Baughman asked at the next commercial break.

While not bothering to turn off the television, he had reduced its drumming volume so that we might be heard.

Keeping my white linen skirt tucked snugly under my knees, I slid a few inches down the church pew in order to move into his peripheral vision.

"My name is Diane Morris, Mr. Baughman. With Anoco Oil Company. I've got something here that belongs to you."

Baughman flicked his bulging blue eyes in my direction, but held his tongue. He waved the remote control at the television screen, lowering the volume an additional two or three increments.

"It's your first royalty payment," I said, trying to avoid looking at his cloven feet.

I flipped open my briefcase and retrieved the green company check. Delivering money is one of the high points of my job; it never fails to produce a memorable moment.

Baughman took the check by the tip of one corner, gave it the most cursory of inspections, then set it down without comment on the padded arm of the recliner. A long pause ensued during which Baughman registered no discernible response. He did not speak, did not flinch or move a muscle; he just sat there staring straight ahead, his feet crossed. I thought perhaps he had lapsed into momentary shock. Just as I was about to summon the housekeeper, Baughman stirred in his recliner.

I have witnessed numerous reactions to large sums of money being suddenly possessed. I have observed grown men and women reduced to weeping hysterics, seen the mean and cynical made to smile. No one but Baughman ever passed gas, at least not in my presence and with such ferocity.

My immediate response was outrage. Pure, unqualified fury. It's as if Baughman intentionally exposed some filthy part of his person merely to humiliate me, study my reaction. I must have flunked the test. I remember feeling a blush of lurid anger from my head to my knees; even the skin of my arms turned crimson. What I really wanted was to slap his ugly ass sideways.

Gathering my briefcase and shoulder bag, I rose to my feet and walked out of the Baughmans' den without a word. I marched in an unwavering straight line through the living room and out the front door, leaving it ajar. But somewhere along the scenic drive from Pointe Claire back home to Baton Rouge, my blinding rage turned to wonder. Here was a man who refused to be buffaloed. Here was a man who, when presented with the palm of great wealth, refused either to grovel or to perform. When the smug oil lady presented the fantastic check, Baughman farted in her face.

On this breezy December morning, unlike our first run-in back in July, Baughman is dressed and out in the yard with his one-eyed dog when I pull into the driveway. Perhaps feeling more sociable than on my initial visit, he ambles over to my parked car and utters a greeting, such as it is.

"Cool enough for you?" he asks.

I wrongfully assume he might make the gentlemanly gesture of opening my car door, but he just stands there gaping as I climb out from behind the wheel. His blatant attempt to peer up my short corduroy skirt is pathetic. His handshake, no surprise, is like clutching a dead fish.

Baughman's most striking physical feature (other than his frightful toes) is his eyes. Unlike most people's, Baughman's eyelids fail to cover his round blue irises, so that when he looks at you, the surrounding whites of his eyes are always showing, making him appear transfixed. Looking at him is like staring at the stars in a Van Gogh painting.

"Good morning, Mr. Baughman. Nice to see you again."

It's a goddamn lie but I've got business to take care of. Baughman nods his head in confirmation that it is indeed nice for me to see him again, but does not respond. When he and his one-eyed dog turn and begin a slow promenade across the front lawn, I follow them.

"I've been visiting with some of your neighbors, Mr. Baughman. I'm trying to determine the ownership to the land beneath Mud Lake. So far it's been a bit of a puzzle."

"I can definitely help you there," he says. "It all belongs to me."

It's Baughman's contention he owns all the property lying under Mud Lake because in late summer of every year, he does.

Mud Lake at Low Water

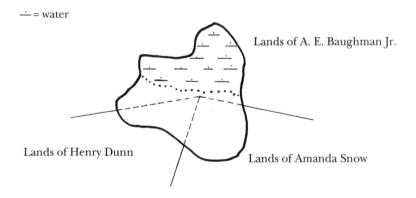

Because for a few weeks in August of every year the water in Mud Lake is located entirely within the boundaries of his property, Baughman wants to claim all the land lying under the lake, regardless of season. He wants the basis of ownership to the lake bottom to be determined at low water. An argument, it seems to me, that is like planting a pecan tree along the border of your property and then forever after claiming not only the fruit, but the free use and benefit of the shade that falls in your neighbor's pasture. It's a lot like getting something for nothing.

"So what you're telling me, Mr. Baughman, is that you claim the entire lake bed, though for eleven months out of the year the water's surface covers parts of your neighbors' property?"

Baughman brings a halt to our rambling tour of his front lawn and turns to face me.

"If the lake bottom is mine," he says, "then all the land lying beneath the lake's surface belongs to me, doesn't it?"

I might have known. No sense of fairness or subtle criticism is going to sway this opponent. He's going to grab everything he can get.

"That's a curious line of logic, Mr. Baughman. Did you know someone has been removing the boundary markers along the shore of Mud Lake?"

Baughman's eyelids flutter, then snap wide open.

"Who told you that?" he says.

"I met with Henry Dunn and Amanda Snow yesterday. They claim someone is removing boundary markers along the lake shore, that someone is trying to take an unfair advantage."

"And you believe that?" he says, favoring me with a smirk. "You believe someone is running around under cover of darkness, digging up boundary markers? Do you really believe that's what this is all about?"

Baughman is a man who plays by his own laws. If he can break your concentration by farting or mocking your reasoning, he wins by forfeit. His little trick is to put people on the defensive, back on their heels answering questions, justifying their comments. It's called rule by intimidation.

"Well, Sir, I can tell you for a fact, no boundary markers are there now. It's unlikely they walked off by themselves."

The one-eyed dog is stopped in his tracks by a weathered pile of feces, possibly his own. Baughman gives the mongrel a boot in the side and the animal backs off.

"Stop playing cops and robbers and use your head," he says. "The issue here is who owns the lake *bottom.* Boundary markers are irrelevant. Those clowns don't know what they're talking about."

"Those markers seem to be causing someone a great deal of concern."

Unable to contain himself, the shepherd noses back toward the mound of excreta only to suffer another kick in the ribs.

"If I were you, Miss," Baughman says out the side of his mouth, "I wouldn't dirty my pretty hands with this lake bottom business. You could get in way over your head. And don't be taken in by some of our more peculiar residents here in Pointe Claire. You might find them amusing, even entertaining, but in the end they'll make an utter fool of you. You take my advice and look out for number one."

Shaking his head in dismissal, Baughman turns on his heel and walks away. The one-eyed dog looks wistfully toward the feces, then follows his master up to the house. The meeting is adjourned.

On the drive back to Baton Rouge, it takes me but a moment to assess the situation. Baughman is determined to claim the entire lake bed despite the possible appeals of his neighbors—even worse, he sees me as someone who might be recruited to pursue his selfish schemes. Amanda Snow and Henry Dunn believe they are being robbed of what's rightfully theirs. My chances of delivering an executed boundary agreement to Anoco Oil Company appear slim to none.

"Other than that," I inform a lone, snow-white bull watching me pass, "everything is just ducky."

six

Back at the office, events move rapidly downhill. My ex-husband Ray telephones to inform me that he will be arriving in Baton Rouge on Thursday afternoon, and he wants the two of us to get together for a drink. No apologies. No explanation of his whereabouts for the past year and a half. No mention of his twelve-year-old son. A true blue asshole through and through.

Ray entered my life at its lowest ebb. I had just blown out my right knee in the fourth game of my senior season at L.S.U., and my basketball-playing days were over. No more summer camps, no more daily practices, no more endless seasons stretching from early fall to middle spring. The sole activity, other than academics, toward which I had devoted my life and affection since the age of eight was taken from me. I was suddenly free to do anything I desired save the one thing I wanted. I staggered around campus on crutches, feeling sorry for myself. Basketball was going its way, I must go mine. I felt lost, cheated. Then I met Ray.

Ray didn't actually work for the Athletic Department but he was always somewhere nearby, hovering in the background. He was not a student, and he was certainly no athlete. He was just an older guy who could help you get a summer job or provide you with extra tickets to big games; he knew everyone connected with L.S.U. athletics on a first-name basis and seemed to have a kind of ill-defined relationship with several prominent booster groups. It was rumored he had ties to a local sports agent.

I was not the most sophisticated of young women. My aspirations entailed dribbling and shooting round balls through orange steel hoops. My focus was on foul shots. Then there was the issue of height, and height had always been an issue in my life. From the time I was in fourth grade, I had been the tallest kid in my elementary school. By my senior year in high school I had shot up to six-feet-four. Say what you will, men have a distinct aversion to laying their heads on a woman's shoulder while dancing, much less being out-rebounded.

Ray never mentioned our considerable difference in height. He was short and dark-eyed with Cajun good looks, and he said he had been watching me from the start. He said he had never seen anyone so long and lovely. On weekends that winter, while my ex-teammates ran up and down the polished wooden court, Ray took me to New Orleans and Mobile and Pensacola. He took me to gambling boats and dog races and cockfights; he wouldn't let me pay for anything. When the weather was clear, we rode in his convertible down the Old Coast Road and waded in the shallow water of the Gulf. Ray walked fast—he was always in a hurry—and I hobbled along behind on my gimp leg. He didn't know the meaning of the word *no*. When I explained that it hurt my knee to lift it, he placed me face down on a pile of pillows and made love to me like no man ever had.

Over the vocal concerns of my parents, Ray and I were married on my twenty-first birthday, four months after we met. We rented a two-bedroom clapboard cottage on Delgado Street not far from the south gates of L.S.U. Ray and I sat up late in the porch swing talking and pondering our future. When the moon was full, we followed its limb-shuttered track across the night sky. Once the neighbors were asleep, we lay a bed of blankets on the brick patio and made love under the dome of trees. Our nakedness hailed the swirling stars.

Tim was born the following winter. Six months later, federal marshals were at the door. Ray and four other men had been arrested and charged with illegal operation of video-poker machines and racketeering. Eventually Ray plea-bargained and was sentenced to eighteen months in a federal prison outside Meridian, Mississippi.

Locked and caged, outfitted in an orange jumpsuit and sandals, all Ray could talk about was getting out, getting free, living a life where no one could ever put a hand on him. The confinement changed him—he grew angry, bitter; sometimes he was afraid. Then the roof fell in.

Ray and several inmates were working off prison grounds in the county courthouse where he was discovered in the basement having sex with one of the secretaries. He was placed in solitary confinement for six weeks, and lost all privileges, including mail. When I next saw him, he insisted I stop visiting. Upon his release, he vanished into thin air.

The entire prison episode made me feel dirty and ashamed. I refused to speak of it to my parents. With Tim, I played a mystery game. I told him how his father was out in the world, seeking his fortune. That one day soon he was going to return from his adventures and all our troubles would be over.

After Ray was paroled, my life became a battle station. I would go months at a time without hearing from him and then he would show up at my door in the middle of the night. He might have a sack full of money and presents for Tim; he might have only the shirt on his back. He might be sober; he might not. He was always desperate for my body. We fell on each other like devils. We locked the doors and pulled the drapes, shutting out everyone and everything. Our lovemaking became ecstatic, untempered, corrupt. We built mansions out of sex, but we couldn't make it last.

"I thought I asked you not to call me here at the office," I say, vowing this time not to let Ray piss me off. "And what gives you the idea I want to have a drink with you?"

"I've missed you, too," Ray says. "My towering goddess of oil."

"Leave me alone, asshole."

So much for keeping my cool. My mistake is trying to deal with Ray straight up, treat him like a regular human being rather than the master tactician he is. He gets me out in the open, then cuts me to pieces.

"I've got several things to tend to while I'm in town, and I thought we should get together," he says. "Meet me at The Chimes at 4:00 on Thursday. We need to talk."

"Listen to me, Ray. There is absolutely nothing left to say. You are dead to me, lost at sea. You don't exist."

It's taken me years to reach this verdict, and I cannot allow it to be overturned by a phone call or the convivial cocktail.

"Thursday at The Chimes," he says, ignoring me. "Our old stomping ground. Do you remember that booth in the back?"

"You make me sick."

If an arrow lodged permanently in the gut is not a serious affliction, I don't know what is.

"Still can't control that nasty temper of yours, can you? The only chink in the armor," he says. "So how goes the hunt for oil?"

"What do you possibly care?"

"You're the mother of my son. I have Tim's welfare to think of."

"You don't care about anybody but yourself."

"You wound me, Diane. I offer my hand and you turn away."

Reject the bait and flee the trap.

"If your hand is out, it's only because you want something."

This last quip found its mark. I can tell.

"You're too smart for me," he says. "But I know your game. The detached idol who keeps everyone at arm's length. Never lets anyone get too close, get inside. Pretending ice water runs in your veins."

"Don't do this, Ray. I have a job, a life, people are counting on me. You can't pop up out of thin air and expect me to just roll over. Least of all *this* week, I haven't got the time. Do me a favor, will you? Go away."

His response is slow in coming and prefaced by nervous laughter.

"That's my girl," he says. "Always running on high throttle. When in doubt, resort to a full-court press. You should try to relax, take life a little easier."

"Is that your advice, Ray? That I should just kick back, let someone else sweat the details? Appreciate what it's like to be a real jerk-off. That's your recommendation?"

"You don't fool me," he says. "You never did."

"Fuck you."

"Now, now, sweetheart, let's not rush into anything. First we talk."

No one ever made me feel more alive, more adored than Ray when we first met. I was twenty; he was dark, handsome and thirty. I was dismayed and crippled and searching. He was bold and enticing and relentless. The better I felt, the more he liked it. All he wanted, he said, was me. All of me.

Ray showered me with affection. He called two, three, four times a day just to check on me. He sent flowers, little gifts whenever he went out of town on business. To this day I own a wooden jewelry box he gave me in celebration of our first month of dating. He would show up unannounced on Friday afternoon and carry me off for the weekend. We stayed in the finest hotels in New Orleans, where Ray ordered champagne and steaks and seafood from room service and our feet seldom touched the gritty, crowded streets below the windows. I spent the better part of many weekends wearing nothing but a red ribbon; for the first time in my life I experienced a man's wide-eyed obsession with my body, his touch, his tongue. If we were to venture out of the hotel, it was to spend the afternoon tucked away in a dark corner of the Napoleon House in the

French Quarter, drinking Sazeracs and holding hands across the table. My head felt filled with helium. At sunset we beat it back to the room.

When we grew tired of the city lights, we made long drives over the back roads of Mississippi. We talked and laughed and sang accompaniment to the radio and drank wine out of paper cups; when the traffic thinned out, Ray ran his hand up my skirt and made me sing solo. We flew over the high piney hills and rode the valleys down, and my heart fell open like a coat.

Maybe it was too good to last. Maybe if I had paid more mind to some of the things Ray was telling me on those long, delirious drives through the Mississippi countryside, I might have gotten a good clue about the future. When a man confides he once made love to four women in four different beds in one raucous night, that he slept with both sisters of his first wife, that he rarely meets a female that doesn't somehow attract him, a prudent woman ought to sit up and take notice. When this same man claims he would crawl naked across an acre of broken glass, swallow swords, just to get to you, a cynical woman would have reason to scoff. But I had never felt the free fall of ecstatic love, and I wanted more.

I am seated at my desk in Anoco's offices. It's after quitting time and yet I remain mulling over today's catalog of endless distractions: a disquieting memo regarding the Pointe Claire boundary dispute from my stressed-out supervisor; two phone calls from Tim about a lost spelling book; a message from Pop reminding me to pick up dog food; the one anxious phone conversation with Ray. I'm not finished: If I don't get to the cleaners I'll have no blouse to wear to work tomorrow; Christmas is two weeks off and I've barely begun shopping; I started my period.

"Give me a goddamn break."

But no such luck.

The memo from my supervisor declares that upper management, without consultation or foresight, has accelerated Pointe Claire's drilling schedule and now wants the exploration department to resolve the troublesome boundary dispute as quickly as possible, like maybe yesterday. My supervisor, his hand ever trembling on the tiller, wants to know if I'm up to the task; if not, why not.

Nor did it escape my attention that several of the old-guard contrarians in the office were sporting self-satisfied sneers all afternoon. They think this is where Wonder Woman finally gets cut down to size. They're all about to pee on themselves.

I sit staring down at the opened Pointe Claire file as if it were about to speak. I've studied it so much I practically have it memorized. My father taught me to approach a problem by first isolating and examining its component parts, trying to get a feel for its underlying nature, who or what's involved, what's at stake, the nature of its genesis, where it might be going, and then just being still, waiting. The solution, Pop preached, will eventually present itself. Often this deduction is less a consequence of how smart you are, which questions you ask or the dint of your will, than it is a measure of how much you can empathize with the root conundrum. How much you care.

All fine and good, but I need answers *now*.

The pending boundary agreement in Pointe Claire Parish provides an excellent trial of Pop's theory of problem solving. My three landowners (Baughman, Amanda Snow, Henry Dunn) are separated not only by their potential economic gain or loss but by long-standing mutual mistrust as well. Henry Dunn has known bigotry, abuse and a kind of second-class citizenship his entire life. Amanda Snow has all but lost everyone (and thereby everything) that ever meant anything to her. Baughman is an unprincipled rascal who happens to be holding most of the cards. There's the quandary; now what are my options?

My first choice would be to concede. Stand up, walk into my supervisor's office and tell him I cannot handle the Pointe Claire project, that I find myself stranded in the middle of an ongoing, acrimonious dispute among a circle of hostile landowners and can discern no feasible resolution. Tell him to put one of the other landmen in the office on the job and allow me to back away.

That is not an option. I'm not backing away from anything.

I could bring in a more aggressive negotiator with hopes of putting pressure on my landowners. Stage a good cop, bad cop routine with me enacting the former role and one of the men in the office taking on the latter. A viable tactic but one that requires starting from scratch and relinquishing some control on my part, neither of which have I time nor inclination for. Besides, I prefer working alone.

I could side with Baughman, the most powerful of my claimants, against Dunn and Snow, the weaker. Backed by Baughman's authority and local connections, I might be able to roll over the confused objections of Dunn and Snow, thereby bringing the boundary dispute to its rapid and desirous conclusion. This remedy, however, would give me no satisfaction. It might please Baughman; it might delight my supervisor and Anoco's upper management, but it would leave me feeling empty. If I wanted a job getting signatures on scattered pieces of paper, I could go to work in a bank.

No, thank you.

I must champion a boundary agreement that will suit all concerned parties, including me.

I don't get home from work until late. The neighborhood looks dark, deserted. As I'm getting out of the car, I notice a figure huddled in the shadows beside the garage.

"Who's there?"

"Oh, it's only me," says Crystal Haygood, emerging in her magic kimono and winter coat.

Is she lying in wait for me? Hoping to ambush Pop? Does the old girl seriously contemplate a romantic tryst here in the side yard? It's the middle of December.

"I know this must look awkward, dear," she says, joining me in the driveway, "but I was thinking of your father."

"Yes," I say, admiring her relentless pluck.

"Tell me," Crystal Haygood says, her eyes glittering. "One woman to another, is he fond of fruit pie? Homemade fruit pie, of course."

Of course. And laced with a fast-acting love potion, no doubt.

"Well, yes, Mrs. Haygood, he likes pie. Is that what's got you out—"

"What kind of pie?" she says, seeming to hover in midair.

Knowing what she wants, the woman gives it her best shot. Watch and take note.

"As far as I know he likes all kinds of pie," I say. "Cherry. Apple. Peach."

"Apple," Crystal Haygood gasps. "I should have known."

Before I can respond, Mrs. Haygood turns and glides across the side yard toward the rear of her house, her feet free of the earth.

"A bunch of sliced apples," she croons, her hands flapping at the ends of her coat sleeves. "A pinch of sweet cinnamon."

Pop had better brace himself.

Tim and Pop have already eaten supper and are seated in the kitchen, the Greek anthology lying open on the table between them. Man and grandson hard at work on the origin of the world.

"After his brother botched the creation of men," Pop says, "Prometheus took over the job."

"Epimetheus gave all the good stuff to the animals," Tim says, reading from the book. "Feathers and fur, wings and shells. Courage, claws, swiftness, a keen sense of smell . . ."

"That left the humans butt-naked and empty-handed," Pop says.

"Not a stitch," Tim says, laughing.

At age twelve, even the remotest allusion to human sexual parts or bodily functions gets a big reaction from Tim. It's a guy thing.

"So then Prometheus took over," Pop says. "He made man in the image of the gods, upright, standing on his two feet."

"Head up, facing the stars," Tim says, his green eyes flashing.

Despite my preference, Tim likes his jet-black hair grown long over his forehead. He gets his hair coloring and fair skin from me. His straight white teeth, like his father's, are perfect.

"Then Prometheus steals fire from Olympus and gives it to the humans," Pop says. "With the possession of fire, man can make weapons and tools, build his shelters and master the animals. Next thing you know he's driving a Cadillac."

Later, once Tim is down for the night, I discover Pop alone in the kitchen. He has trouble sleeping most nights and spends the wee hours holed up in here, drinking coffee, digging in the fridge, rattling the pots and pans. It's like living with a troop of raccoons.

"Tough day?" he asks.

"I've had better," I reply. "And much worse. What about you?"

Pop is seated at the table, aligning rows of photographs of my mother across the flat surface. The pictures bring back the well of sadness surrounding her death. It's like a sock in the stomach.

"You work too hard," he says, studying me.

"No more than anyone else."

"I'm your father," he says. "I've been watching you since the day you were born."

"It's my job, Pop. It's my job and I get paid for it. It's why they call it work."

"Nothing you've ever done was just a job or just a game or just a hobby," he says. "You won't let go until something gives."

There's no sense trying to temper the mental image playing in Pop's mind. To him, I ride a tall white stallion and never fail to hit the bull's-eye. It's flattering, but untrue.

I duck into the laundry room off the kitchen and transfer wet clothes from the washer to the dryer. From the dirty clothes hamper, I refill the washer with a load of whites, add soap and spin the dial.

"I haven't seen you wear that outfit in ages," Pop says, looking up from the rows of photographs aligned on the table.

The outfit is my basketball warmup suit from my playing days at L.S.U. It's purple nylon with gold stripes down the sleeves and pants legs; my name stitched in big gold letters across the back. My number: 44. The suit is cotton-lined and warm, and wearing it always reminds me of less trying times when I had only myself and the opposing team with which to contend.

I know it's probably unwise to give Pop too much information, but at the moment I've nowhere else to turn. Besides, you move in with me and you take your chances.

"It's Ray, Pop. He's coming to Baton Rouge on Thursday. He says he wants to talk."

"Sounds great," he says, without missing a beat. "I've got a couple of matters I've been dying to talk with Ray about. Two minutes is all I ask."

My father would make a formidable opponent. Though twenty-five years his junior, Ray would find himself smothered in the arms of a great grizzly bear impassioned by the defense of its own.

"I'm sure he wants something, Pop. I don't know if it's money or a place to lay low for a while or what. From the sound of it, he's out of work again."

Pop is at heart a gentle man and a malicious smile does not sit well upon his countenance.

"Provided anyone could ever call gambling and card playing a full-time job," he says.

"It's Tim that worries me. If Ray wants to see Tim, I don't know what to do."

"He's got no legal right," Pop says. "Tell him *I* said that."

"Tim is his son."

Pop rummages through the shoe box of family snap-shots sitting in his lap and selects a photograph. After a close examination, he positions it with the others on the table. An exaggerated sense of control is one way he keeps his emotions in check.

"No," he says. "He lost all custodial rights years ago. He lost all moral and natural rights when he abandoned his family for years without so much as a phone call. Everyone is better off without him."

"What am I to say to Tim?"

Pop sets the shoe box on the floor and lays his hands flat on the table.

"Tell Tim his father died in a foreign land. That he died trying to get back to his family, that the last word on his tongue was Tim's name."

"You know I can't tell him that."

"I know," he says.

Pop pulls a chair away from the table and clears a space free of photographs.

"Come sit," he says.

"What's wrong, Pop?" I say, sitting down beside him.

"Wrong?" he says.

He selects a photograph from the stack on the table and holds it up for me to see. It's a picture of my mother taken when she was in college. She is young and beautiful and a wild ecstasy burns in her eyes. It's my all-time favorite picture of her. Pop studies the picture, then looks at me.

"You know what I miss the most?" he says. "I miss the sound of her voice."

"It's all right, Pop," I say, laying my fingers on the spotted backs of his hands. "I miss her, too."

The photograph falls out of Pop's hand onto the floor.

He makes no move to retrieve it. There is nothing to say and yet I am compelled to speak.

"We have to believe it's for the best, Pop. We have to believe it's for reasons we're not able to see."

"I cannot believe that," he says, rearing back in his seat. "I won't be placated with weary clichés for the old and dying. There are no gods and no goddesses."

I cannot speak to my father's despairing view of the sublime. With a full-time job, an impressionable young son and a widowed parent on my hands, I have no time for formal speculation. It's all moving so fast. This morning I found myself standing half dressed in the center of my closet unable to remember which day of the week it was. Or what I once wanted to do in life.

Slow down, my father counseled when I was growing up, slow down if you want to move quickly.

PART III

Wednesday

seven

Arriving at my desk, I find four phone messages waiting, all of them frantic and all from A. E. Baughman Jr. I had hoped for a better start to the day.

"We've got trouble, Miss, right here in Pointe Claire Parish! I recommend you drop whatever you're doing and get up here. *Pronto.* If you can't handle this Mud Lake business, we'll have to find us someone who can. You hear?"

The mere sound of his voice makes me want to barf.

I cross the new bridge over the Mississippi and pick up the levee road outside Port Allen. Above the open cane fields, flocks of egrets, like pieces of white confetti, flutter in the thin air. Below the small town of Crossroads, seat of Pointe Claire Parish government, I turn onto the Boone Road, a gravel-topped drive through a procession of grass pastures and pecan orchards. Round-eyed cattle stand in erratic clusters, looking forlorn and forgotten—a nation of friendless brutes.

Baughman is standing beside a sheriff's patrol car when

I pull into his driveway. I can feel his riveting X-ray vision trying to contain my thoughts. I'm tempted to walk over and crown him with my shoulder bag.

"One small shot for womankind," I mumble, "one giant headache for man."

Delightful daydream, but one that must be rejected for now.

"Better late than never," Baughman says when I join him in the driveway.

"Good morning," I say through gritted teeth.

Baughman ignores my salutation and gestures toward the figure sitting in the patrol car.

"Miss, this is Sheriff Price," he says. "Morris is with the oil company, Sheriff. She's the one trying to clear up that lake bottom business I was telling you about."

Sheriff Price is a sorrowful-looking man in his mid-thirties who fills much of the front seat of his patrol car. He's not overweight, he's just big, big-boned, with huge hands and shoulders and a barrel chest. He has a reflective, downcast bent to his appearance. He strikes me as a man who, knowing trouble when he sees it, has recently seen some of it.

"Morning," says the sheriff, enveloping my extended hand in his and squeezing.

"Miss, I want you to take a little ride with me and the sheriff," Baughman says, taking full command. "There's something you need to see. Get in."

With no space available in the front of the patrol car, Baughman and I climb into the backseat. The front seat, what's not consumed by the person of Sheriff Price, is occupied by a stunning array of crime-fighting equipment. There's two telephones, a police radio, a white cowboy hat, a walkie-talkie, a mysterious black box the size of a kitchen toaster, a radar gun, a bullhorn, a dashboard-mounted computer with twitching dials and black cables. It's like looking into the cockpit of a combat jet.

With the sheriff behind the wheel, the patrol car circles behind the ranch house and picks up a gravel lane that leads a quarter mile through the bare winter woods onto a wide plateau, the site of Baughman's new horse barn. In the final phase of its construction, the twenty-thousand-square-foot, cement-floored, climatically controlled, steel and heavy-gauge aluminum structure is better designed and more equipped than many of the homes and office buildings in this country parish.

Sheriff Price pulls round behind the new barn and stops the patrol car. Freshly scrawled in dripping black paint across the barn's entire back wall reads the inscription:

YOU CAN RUN BUT YOU CAN'T HYDE!!

"They don't know who they're fooling with," says Baughman, bending forward to look out the patrol car's windshield.

"Who doesn't know?" I ask, hoping for enlightenment.

Baughman turns to face me on the backseat, his eyeballs whirling in their sockets.

"Miss, you're beginning to worry me," he says. "Can't you see what's happening here? They're trying to get to me by threatening my property. They think for the price of a gallon of paint, I'll give up what's rightfully mine."

Baughman's speech betrays a jot of anxiety beneath his bravado. A hairline crack of weakness running through the central core. Perhaps it's something I can use against him.

"Who are *they*, Mr. Baughman? And what is it they want you to surrender?"

"It's this Mud Lake business," he says, shaking his head in disgust. "Some of my neighbors want to influence my thinking. They think I'll falter at the sight of a little black paint. They have vivid imaginations."

Baughman's own imagination appears to be operating at full tilt.

"You think Amanda Snow and Henry Dunn are responsible for this?" I ask.

"I believe they would do anything that might help their cause," he says. "Even if it meant removing their own boundary markers. Or defacing my property. And I'm not the only one who thinks so. Am I, Sheriff?"

Sheriff Price sits in the front seat gripping the steering wheel, looking as if he's eaten some bad food.

"Sheriff," I say, leaning forward on the backseat, "you don't really believe Amanda Snow is responsible for something like this, do you? Or Henry Dunn? He's seventy-four years old."

Sheriff Price sits still, alternately clenching his left and right fists round the steering wheel. The big blue veins on the backs of his hands rise to the surface and then disappear, rise and then disappear.

"I've known Amanda Snow since I was six years old," he says calmly. "When she gets it in her head, she's one of the most contrary persons you'll ever meet. I wouldn't underestimate her."

"And Henry Dunn?" I say. "You think he would do something like this?"

The sheriff takes his hands off the steering wheel and lays them on the sunlit dash. He drums his powerful fingers and sighs.

"Henry Dunn is one of the craftiest people I know," he says. "He'll trick you into thinking he's a harmless old fool, all the while he's laughing behind your back. And his three sons are no different."

"You've had trouble with them?" I ask.

Sheriff Price's solemn brown eyes meet mine in the rearview mirror. A hot flash runs down my spine.

"Henry Dunn and I once crossed swords over the rightful ownership of a stray cow," he says. "It's a long story."

"A long story with a sad ending," Baughman says. "I had an interest in that cow, too!"

"The altercation over the cow happened some time ago," the sheriff says. "Not long after I took over the department. We've put it behind us now."

"I can tell you one goddamn thing," Baughman says, "that black paint didn't jump on that barn by itself. Sheriff, it's your job to protect life and property in this parish. I don't think we need a master detective to see who's behind all this. If you need the names and addresses of the most likely suspects, I'll be happy to give them to you."

Before Sheriff Price can reply, Baughman throws open the door on his side of the patrol car and climbs out.

"Miss," he says, "let's you and I take a little walk."

Off a short plank. Lucky me.

There are moments when I just want to kiss it off. Walk away and get another job, something nine to five with an hour off for lunch, nights and weekends free. Let someone else lead the charge for oil, battle the craving beasts.

The urge to chuck it all passes in a few minutes, though. It occurs most often when I'm under stress, backed into a corner, sick of landowners and their incessant demands. If I offer them a hundred dollars an acre to lease their land, they want a hundred and ten; agree to pay them twenty percent royalty, they want twenty-two percent. No offer is ever good enough. Their mantra goes: What have you done for me lately?

What I'm really selling is an idea: greed. Greed is my business. *Lease your land to me, Mr. Brown, and you'll make more money than you ever dreamed! Sign this paper and you might get fucking rich!* Like I've got some kind of insider, Midas touch. Lucky charms and voodoo simmering in my purse. People stop me on country roads and demand I take down their names and box numbers. I'm the living prospect of wealth, wildcat wells and the good life. Perfect strangers call me Ma'am and doff their hats. Young children giggle and stare out from behind their mothers at the oil lady.

Hush, child! I'm talking to the oil lady.

Admittedly, there are some unintended perks of the trade. Blessed by the windfall of oil money, many landowners respond in kind. Grateful farmers load me down with sacks of sweet potatoes, yellow onions, mustard greens, ripe tomatoes, fresh okra, butter beans, ears of corn, flats of strawberries. I've been known to fetch home gifts of pork sausage, venison, geese, ducks, boudin, shrimp, blue crabs, catfish fillets, Black Angus steaks. A little prosperity brings out the best in everybody.

And then periodically I run up against a person like Baughman. Baughman's brain is so finely wired that not getting precisely what he wants never occurs to him. His style of negotiating is to dictate what terms he will accept. Just give him all he wants and he's quite congenial, even kind.

The fact is, I cannot compel an unwilling landowner to do anything. I have no tangible sway over him, no powers of coercion or authority; I cannot produce a weapon and demand he comply with my wishes or sign my document. I can only hope to make him see my proposal in light of a larger picture, that what I bring to the table may be to his ultimate boon. I may lead, I may charm, but I cannot command.

I crawl out my side of the patrol car and shut the door. Sheriff Price runs his window down, motioning me closer. He seems less agitated now that Baughman has left the vehicle, more solicitous. Even his woeful brown eyes have lightened.

"A word of advice, Miss Morris," he says. "Often the difference between the good guys and the bad guys is only a matter of degree."

"Meaning exactly what, Sheriff?"

He looks in the rearview mirror and drums his fingers on the dash. Like it or not, he appears to be getting drawn into something he wants no part of.

"Watch what you say, be careful who you trust," he says. "I'll be right here if you need me."

The sheriff runs his window back up and gets on the radio. Whatever he knows or suspects, he's not willing to speak of it. At least for now.

I catch up to Baughman and follow him around to the front of the horse barn. From within the cavernous building come the sporadic sounds of finish carpentry, the casual rhythms of workmen in the final days of a major construction. Baughman stops in the barn's open doorway and looks out across the sprawling landscape. In the distance stand the stout levee walls holding back the Mississippi. The river makes a huge bend in this part of Pointe Claire, bordering Baughman's extended property on three sides.

Baughman puts his hands in his coat pockets and rocks back on his heels. Ready or not, I'm about to get an earful. Stand still and listen up.

"The land here is everything," Baughman says. "Without this land there's no sugarcane or bean fields or beef cattle or thoroughbred horses. No fancy barns, no ranch house."

"No money from oil wells," I say, cutting him off.

Baughman turns and glares as if heeding me for the first time. I hold my ground and stare back.

"That's right, Miss," he says finally, "and no money from oil wells. This land is everything. My father fought, connived, suffered and lived for it. What he couldn't buy outright, he traded for or stole. He poured his heart and soul into this place. If you think I'm going to voluntarily give up one square foot of it, you are sadly mistaken."

"You're referring to the land beneath Mud Lake?"

"I have no intention of giving it up," he says flatly.

Having said his piece, Baughman appears satisfied to stand and watch the cattle graze. But it's all too pat, too easy. What's needed is someone to jerk his chain.

"May I point out, Sir," I say firmly, "that technically, the land under the lake is not yours to *give up*."

Baughman receives the news like a sound thump on the nose. He puts one hand into a pocket of his khaki slacks and jiggles the loose change.

"Like my father," he says, regaining control of his anger, "I'm accustomed to getting what I want, when I want it. And like my father, I'm not above showing a measure of gratitude when it pleases me to do so. I understand that everyone needs to feel compensated, that in the end we all look out for ourselves. I can be very generous, Miss."

It's all coming out now. I ready myself before playing the next card.

"What could I possibly do for you?" I say, accompanied by the faintest trace of a smile.

Baughman casts one goggle-eye in my direction. Time he put up or shut up.

"You are in a position of some authority with this lake bed business," he says. "You seem to have the confidence of my neighbors. You might be inclined to support conclusions, promote certain points of view. They will listen to you."

Reaching the nadir of his sales pitch, Baughman steps closer to me. His bad breath and snide expression make me want to back away, but I don't. I wouldn't give him the pleasure.

"I'm prepared to make it worth their while," he says, giving full rein to his scheming nature. "I'll buy the land if that's what they want. You have them agree to a reasonable figure, and I'll pay them for it. This is simply a business matter, Miss. The way I see it, it's the cost of doing business."

Baughman nods his head collaboratively, as if this were a game at which the two of us were old hands. But I've been down this road before.

"Paying them for the present value of the land is meaningless, Mr. Baughman. You would be offering pennies for what might be worth thousands of dollars. Maybe more."

"Perhaps," he says, his eyes spinning, "but then no one knows that for sure, do they? You do what you can to help me, Miss, and I'll see what I can do to help you."

He took his slow sweet time but there it is: a tall white bag of sugar candy lying unattended on the table. All I have to do is reach out and take it. Though not a surprise, the immediacy of the bribe is like catching a whiff of something dead.

"My job is to promote a compromise among all the landowners," I say. "Do you really expect your neighbors to sign a boundary agreement that is not to their advantage?"

"I expect them to do right by me," he says, "and I'll do right by them."

"Which is another way of saying, Sir, what's good for you is good for them."

In a less heated moment, I might have used a different tack, toned it down a bit. But it's past that.

Baughman pauses for a split second, then switches his oscillating eyeballs to full-freaky power. He rattles the loose change in his pants pocket.

"Pointe Claire is a special kind of place," he says slowly. "It's not like the city, not like one of your richer parishes. It's peaceful here, things move slowly, everybody knows who you are, what you do, what kind of people you come from. We don't favor a lot of agitation in our daily affairs. We ask folks to do what's expected of them, mind their own business, and everyone will get along just fine."

Baughman's tone of voice is now subdued, confident, as if we were two old friends comparing notes on farm prices. Like the sun and rain, he takes my collusion as a matter of course. I'm just another commodity to be bought and traded. Wonder how he might react to being hit in the face with a gob of hot spit.

"I'm not here to pass judgment on the dynamics of Pointe Claire society, Mr. Baughman. Or make friends or extort money or take sides. I'm here to negotiate a boundary agreement."

"But while you are here," he says, leaning closer to me, "while you are among us, you will conduct yourself in an agreeable manner. You will do that, pretty Miss, or I will have you run out of this parish."

eight

Driving back to Baton Rouge by way of the river road, I turn up the car's heater and lower the windows. Let the cold air rush in; allow my rattled reflections to peek out.

It's clear that though he is still reluctant to talk of compromise, Baughman is running scared. Why else would he threaten me? If he really thought he could end all inquiry into this Mud Lake business, then why doesn't he just run me out of the parish?

Because it's not that simple. Because Baughman knows if he were to get rid of me, Anoco would only send someone else to Pointe Claire to finish the job. Besides, I think he likes his chances with me. He's studied the playing field, assessed all the combatants, and now believes he can cajole, browbeat me into advancing his cause. In his view, I am an outsider and a woman, neither of which counts for much.

The situation with my ex-husband Ray is more complicated. Whereas Baughman poses an obstacle to the performance of my job, Ray has the potential to destroy my entire life and everyone close to it. Ray is the bad dream that won't go away. Rather, Ray is a nightmare that goes away for months, sometimes years, only to return. For a time.

I remember once finding a motel room key in a pocket of Ray's pants. This was when we were still living together on Delgado Street, before the arrival of the federal marshals. Why would a man who rents a house just south of the L.S.U. campus have the need of a nearby motel room? When I confronted him, Ray didn't so much as wince.

"Look, Diane, my work takes me all across the Gulf coast. I wake up in one town, eat lunch in another, and go to sleep in still another. I like to move fast, and I like to travel light. You're just going to have to deal with that."

"What you mean is, I just have to get used to it," I said. "Trust the man who once bragged to me of sleeping with half the women in south Baton Rouge."

The Delgado house sat under an unbroken canopy of live oak trees. The arching black limbs shut out the heat and sunlight, bathing the house and patio in perpetual shadow. Ray sat in the porch swing under the revolving fan blades in shorts and no shirt. He rubbed his flat stomach and smiled thinly.

"Well, Diane," he said. "It's a small town."

Arriving at the outskirts of Baton Rouge, I find the new bridge over the Mississippi has been closed due to a flaming car accident, rerouting all east-west interstate travel over the old Huey Long bridge. Traffic is backed up all over town. Truckers and motorists from Texas, Florida,

California, Georgia suddenly find themselves stalled in the midst of our fair city. It takes me an hour to get to my home in Southdowns. There in the driveway when I arrive is Crystal Haygood, resplendent as usual in her blue kimono. In her oven-mittened hands rests a freshly baked pie.

"For your father," she says, blushing. "It's apple. I hope he likes it."

"It's his favorite, Mrs. Haygood. He'll be speechless. Let's go in together."

In the kitchen, we find Pop and Tim poised over their mythology books, the remainders of an after-school snack littering the table top. As if prodded by the still-bubbling pie, Pop is quickly to his feet, backpedaling across the room.

"Now, Crystal, you shouldn't have," he says. "It's too much. Much too much."

"It's no bother, Richard," she says. "No bother at all."

Spending as much time as I do away from the house, I had no idea these two had reached a first-name basis. Mrs. Haygood's romantic perseverance is paying dividends.

"I like baking for a man. And handsome boys, too," she says, including Tim in her wide net.

"A pie," Tim says. "Can I have some?"

"Later," I say.

Mrs. Haygood's daring frontal attack has overwhelmed Pop's normally stalwart defenses. He's backed up against the fridge with his mouth open. A man in headlong retreat.

"It's very kind of you to think of us," I say. "Pop likes cheddar cheese melted on his apple pie."

"A cheese man," Mrs. Haygood says breathlessly. "You don't see too many of those anymore."

"Cheese," Pop says, beginning to pant.

Though this is great fun to watch, I better lend my outmatched father a hand.

"I know we will all enjoy the pie, Mrs. Haygood," I say. "Just set it there on the counter. We'll have it for dessert."

"Next time I'll bring along the cheese," she says, giving Pop a leering wink.

"Cheese," he says, only it sounds more like *Jeeze*.

I take Mrs. Haygood by the arm and lead her out of the kitchen. In the foyer, she pulls me close.

"Do you think he'll like it?" she whispers.

"Take my word for it," I say, easing her out the front door. "There's nothing in this world he likes better than homemade apple pie."

"I wouldn't touch that pie with a ten-foot stick!" Pop says upon my return to the kitchen. "It's the thin end of the wedge. You couldn't pay me to touch it."

"I want some," Tim says.

"Turncoat," Pop says.

"After your supper," I tell Tim.

Of my two parents, Pop was most vociferous in his dislike for Ray. He tried everything within his power to keep us from dating after we first met. He counted out the reasons Ray was not the man for me.

"One," Pop said, "he's Cajun with a Cajun mentality."

"What does *that* mean, Pop? Are you going to start profiling my friends by race and ethnic group? Their hair color?"

"Two. He's all talk," Pop said. "All talk and sly smiles."

"Look who's talking."

"Three. He thinks he can worm his way into any place he wants. I wouldn't trust him to walk my dog."

Little did Pop know. Ray was beyond walking the dog and had already paid a visit to my room in L.S.U.'s women's athletic dorm, off-limits to all non-students. And I had helped him.

Ray's proposal was as simple as it was risqué. After I detailed the exact location of my first-floor dorm window, Ray suggested that he appear there in the dark of night and scratch on the screen.

"I'll scratch on the screen," he said, "and you'll let me in."

Once my heart stopped racing, I started to itch.

The women's athletic dorm—though injured I was still on scholarship—lay catercornered to the varsity tennis courts and beside a grove of perpetually green pine and live oak trees. A suitor, were he so bold, might slip across the wooded area and approach the northernmost wing of the dorm after visiting hours with little chance of being seen. If he knew exactly which window he was heading for and had a prearranged signal with the young woman residing within, he could walk up and step through the unlatched screen without even breaking stride.

Welcome, brave stranger, step in and be welcome.

The best part of the story comes later when Ray, who had built his courage around several tall glasses of draft beer, was forced to relieve himself. Rather than stepping half-dressed back into the cold outside my window, Ray chose to slip into the girls' rest room just down the hall. And if a junior high jumper named Wanda Velker—a strict Baptist from Waterproof, Louisiana—had not obeyed the call of nature at more or less the same instant, everything might have gone smoothly. But when Wanda looked down and saw the two bare, hairy and unladylike feet in the stall next to her, she let go a shriek that broke the peace of that starry winter night.

Somehow Ray managed to get out of the bathroom stall,

back down the hall to my room and out the window without confronting more wandering coeds. But it was his great misfortune to run half-dressed across the wide parking lot into the passing high-beam headlights of campus security at just that moment in time. And campus security always gets its man.

Even under intense police questioning, Ray refused to alter his story or confess that he had any knowledge of a non-student invasion of the women's athletic dorm or of any female resident who might have offered assistance to the confusion that followed. He claimed he had been out for a late-night jog. The university authorities were convinced otherwise but had no proof. Eventually, they let the smooth-talking suspect go.

Things a woman cannot discuss with her father: sex; waking wet in the night; an aching vaginal tightness; recurring dreams of straddling her ex-husband; ovulation; masturbation; first sex; most recent sex; favorite fantasies; periods; birth control; oral sex; orgasms. Pop and I are compadres, best of buddies but there are healthy, well-prescribed limits. I have not a clue what sexual yearnings arise in his mind. No wish to go there.

Ray's unsanctioned visit to my college dorm room was not my first sexual interlude; the first occurred at age eight. Though non-consummating, it was nonetheless unforgettable. The whole thing happened in a flash and only much later came back to me through a series of lurking intuitions, like breaking a long-cherished thumbnail and for days afterward feeling the frustration though the hurt of the initial event fades away.

My mother and I were visiting my aunt in Houston, Texas, during the Easter holidays. Aunt Jennifer was loud, crass and redheaded, and never ceased running her mouth. To my aunt's favor, she had a fourteen-year-old son named Stan who was blue-eyed and handsome, and I was mightily smitten. One morning Stan walked into the living room where I was reading and took a seat at the opposite end of the couch. From the depths of his glowing blue eyes emitted a sly, provocative gaze. In the center of his open palm rested a small jar of colorless liquid in which (he declared) floated his recently extracted tonsils. It was at that point that my profound ignorance and slumbering sexuality became tangled. How, at age eight, did I have the first inkling of what constituted a ribald manner on the part of a fourteen-year-old boy? Why did I necessarily assign a sexual connotation (whatever that was) to something as bizarre as a pair of tonsils bobbing in a vial of clear alcohol? What, for Pete's sake, were tonsils?

The physical attraction between girl and boy originates beneath the mere clamor of words and phrases and is not unlike a mild upset stomach. The alluring look of a fourteen-year-old male is the bold stare into the soul of his younger female cousin, and her subsequent realization that that might account for the butterflies swarming inside her abdomen. Tonsils are two chunks of gristly-looking flesh about the size of grapes taken from a dark place inside an older boy's body. A secret is when he wants her to examine them.

I couldn't have been more surprised if Stan had reached behind the couch and produced his mother's red severed head.

Following our supper of grilled shrimp and salad, Pop summons Tim and me to the den to witness television's latest foray into the surreal. Yesterday's vapid offerings eclipsed by today's unspeakable crimes. Earlier this afternoon, a Baton Rouge native barricaded himself and two female hostages in a downtown bank building where he now awaits the end of everything. Or is it the bloody beginning?

State and local law enforcement have surrounded the Acadian State Bank, severing all communications save for one phone line that allows a running dialogue with the renegade bank customer. TV cameras have tapped into the building's surveillance system, providing continuous video coverage from inside the bank lobby. Sound trucks and news teams have fanned out across the central business district, satellite dishes sprouting like toadstools amid the downtown streets. Events are now being carried live across the country via cable news channels.

Pop, Tim and I sit in silence and watch as a succession of local officials appear on the TV screen, deploring the deepening drama. The passersby peering into the cameras are our friends and colleagues; a sense of alarm mingled with sudden notoriety has swept the capital city.

"A judgment on this sullied house!" cries the bomb-wielding agonist. "Den of hustlers, avarice and shame."

Authorities have identified the assailant as a former marine commando, master of explosives and veteran of numerous overseas operations, recently relieved of duty and returned home to peacetime Baton Rouge. Neighbors describe him as withdrawn, a loner, an agitated ex-warrior with no future and nothing to lose.

"No ordinary lunatic," Pop observes. "Here's a man capable of wreaking havoc on a grand scale."

Striking a chord among the ranks of more belligerent viewers, the ex-commando enjoyed an initial groundswell of unspoken, grudging support, the proud combatant pitted against the corporate tyrant. Righter of grievous wrongs.

But once the public learned of his battery of bombs and incendiary devices, the presence of the women hostages, all allegiance evaporated. He squats alone in his seething wrath, ranting into the telephone.

"Bloodsuckers! Dog's heart! Usurious vermin! Swine. Fiend who feeds on its people. You've taken everything and left me nothing. Obscene church of profit!"

The ex-soldier's fuming aggression is directed toward the bank and its punitive lending policies. He demands the prompt return of all unjustly seized assets and the names and particulars of all responsible; he wants the guilty punished. He seeks a face-to-face confrontation with Acadian's board of directors.

"It's the dark vision of our friend Achilles," Pop says, shaking his head in dismay, "still living among us after all these centuries. Lover of battle, the bravest and the best, the hero, the killer, never more brilliant than when making war, sowing chaos."

"Why won't they meet with him?" Tim asks, mesmerized by the frightful circus. "At least talk to him and see what he wants, see if they can work something out."

"He's got what he wants," I tell him. "He's got us all watching."

"But he's never going to get away with it," Tim protests. "He's surrounded; there's no escape."

"It's not about getting away with anything," Pop says, staring at the television screen. "It's all about rage, vengeance. Gone is the spectacle of the lone fanatic throwing himself off a tower or a bridge or beneath the wheels of a passing train to highlight his misfortune. These days the goal seems to be how much carnage they can leave behind."

The television cameras pan slowly across the glittering downtown area, the hushed state capitol, the evacuated agencies of government and public welfare, its law courts, its churches, the empty streets and abandoned temples of finance, all powerless now before the specter of one man's passion.

"At a time that cries out desperately for a hero," Pop says, "all that emerges is a procession of enraged villains."

After more than five hours since the mid-afternoon takeover, tensions outside the bank building appear to be reaching a climax. TV news teams scamper back and forth across lines of barricades, their strained faces, their grim reporting tinged with a terrible beauty. Small squads of helmeted and heavily armed police officers are seen marching in lockstep to their stations; platoons of expert marksmen peer down from the rooftops, moonlight glancing off their blue-black armaments. Cops in cars, in buses, in pickup trucks and helicopters. Cops on foot, on motorcyles, on bicycles, on horses. The vicious finale is scripted. Inside the bank the lone warrior has lost none of his boundless fury, his periodic cries echoing off the marbled lobby walls.

"You have cheated and deceived me. You will not beguile me!"

Tim sits gaping, enthralled by the unfolding panorama, the thrill of the chase, the hint of catastrophe. He licks his dry lips and waits. For once, Pop is at a loss for words.

"It's all wrong," I say, breaking the spell. "This is no standoff, no stalemate. It's an execution. The old soldier crossed over the line, hit his nemesis where he lives, and now they're going to kill him for it. Or he kills himself. And the two women die either way. Out here in the open and the whole world gets to watch."

Without warning the would-be avenger is seen emerging into the blinding array of television lights illuminating the empty bank lobby. In his gloved right hand he holds some sort of gadget from which trail numerous black wires. He grins and slowly raises his hand high above his head. And then, before the unflinching eye of the cameras, the entire glass front of the bank building detonates beneath a vortex of automatic gunfire; flying glass and muzzle blasts light the city streets; two terrific explosions followed by huge jets of molten flames flower into the sky. Frantic screams of men and women peal through the night; swarms of special police units are sent storming through windows, doors, skylights. In thirty seconds it is finished. His body hit with as many as twenty-five explosive rounds, the ex-marine's corpse is shown gutted and dismembered, empty of venom, void of meaning, his black blood spattering the lobby floor. Three policemen are seriously injured, numerous bystanders hit by flying glass; the two female hostages dead where they lie.

The slaughter is swift, final and complete; the curious viewing of it depraved. I feel sick, disgusted, culpable.

Tim is mute with horror.

"No winners here, no heroes," Pop mutters, the despoiled bank burning on the television screen. "None honored save the angels of violence."

Later, alone in my bed, I cannot chase the appalling images of the bank fiasco out of my mind. Was it doomed to end in bloodshed? Did the ex-soldier feel so much as a shred of concern for anyone other than his outraged self? Was it imperative the authorities bring their entire arsenal of death to bear? Must aggression always be met measure for measure?

Though hardly credible in light of the tragic events surrounding the scene at the bank, I cannot help thinking of my own life-sized enemies: A. E. Baughman Jr., my ex-husband Ray. What are the self-imposed limits we must erect when opposing those who threaten us? Does the end ever justify the means? What are my options? Both men mean me mischief; both men mean to put something over on me. Both mean to have their way. A showdown with each seems fated, unavoidable; I can only vow to keep my senses. Hope to keep the conflict from spiraling out of control.

PART IV

Thursday

nine

I sleep soundly through the night until just before daylight when I wake from a dream in which I am dead. In my nightmare I am walking alone down a windowless, white-painted corridor. The floor, walls and low-slung ceiling of the narrow passageway are audibly humming, as if encased with electronics and life-support systems. At the end of the hallway is an unmarked door. Part of my mind is in open flight.

Don't do it! Don't touch that door! Go outside and play!

But just like the heroines in old horror movies, I keep going. Naturally the door opens without me even touching it, granting access to the brightly lighted room beyond. The room itself is as big as a small gymnasium, with bare rectangular walls and a ceiling that disappears into blackness above glaring fluorescent lights. Large flasks of percolating chemicals, coils of glass tubing, bubbling beakers sit atop the laboratory counters that partition the room into long aisles of equal length. Piles of what look to be soiled bed linens are strewn pell mell about the floor. Parked here and there at odd angles are a dozen or so empty hospital beds. Masked and gloved technicians come and go without acknowledgment—a bustling beehive of peculiar research. From somewhere above or behind the walls of the great room come the echoing shrieks of countless voices, the thundering of stamping feet and clapping hands, a wailing, swirling cascade of human grief and agitation, as if the lower chamber lies beneath a packed sports arena wherein the home team is being vanquished or some unspeakable hell is being witnessed. The spectators' unrestrained agony is manifest.

Off in a far corner of the great room, face up on one of the unattended hospital beds, I find my body. Curiously, my initial reaction is not one of terror but lamentation. To have lived this long, to have seen and heard and felt so much, to have hoped for so much, only to come to death. Under the fluorescent lights my skin looks blue and flaccid. The frozen scowl on my face bespeaks a sentiment beyond the living.

I wake in the dim light of my bedroom, a fine glaze of fear-laden sweat dampening the sheets. To move forward, to get on with my private life, to see this Pointe Claire business to its rightful end, I must first overcome myself. To resist, to shy away, to falter, is to risk the ruin of all.

Over breakfasts of eggs and fried ham, Pop and Tim recount the finer points of heroism.

"To the Greeks, life was all about excellence," Pop says, mopping yellow yolk with buttered toast. "Not duty to country or to others but rather duty to *oneself*. A devotion to wit, courage, honor, excellence. Bold of heart, nimble of mind."

"And being the best fighter," Tim says, inspired by his grandfather's ardor.

"Best fighter, best talker, best thinker, bravest leader, best father in the land," Pop says.

He gives me a curt little nod lest I've forgotten his contempt for my ex-husband Ray. To Pop, Ray is the feral dog nosing round the door, a guileful monster devoid of character or the capacity for love. In Pop's mind, a man, a hero, is someone who goes forth alone into the labyrinth of the world and finds himself, becoming all the better for it.

"And these Greek heroes of yours?" I ask. "I suppose they were big eaters as well?"

Pop's eyes slide guiltily back to his nearly empty breakfast plate.

"By the way," I ask, "who polished off the rest of Mrs. Haygood's apple pie?"

The ensuing moment of silence is cavernous.

"I got hungry during the night," Pop says.

He excuses his nocturnal pie eating with a wave of one hand.

"I thought you said you wouldn't touch that pie with a ten-foot—"

"It would have been rude to let it go to waste," he says.

"Well, you know what they say, Pop? The best way to a man's heart is through—"

"I think we've had enough idle chatter this morning," he says, bringing his breakfast things to the sink. "Some of us have chores to do."

And dragons to slay.

I cross the Mississippi by way of the reopened new bridge from Baton Rouge. The smoldering ruins of the Acadian State Bank, like the remnants of communal grief, still dirty the downtown sky. Beneath the bridge, the Mississippi is running high and fast. The stiff current ripples the water's surface, shattering the bright sunlight into points of white fire.

Today's mission to Pointe Claire is to gather information. With no breakthrough on the Mud Lake boundary agreement in sight, I feel a need to learn more about the players. To that end, my plan is to first pay a visit to the offices of Sheriff Price, keeper of the peace.

The parish sheriff in this state is the chief law enforcement official. Most holders of that high office tend to be men of the more wizened variety, with long histories in positions of local authority and public trust. By these standards, Sheriff Price is a dashing young star.

Thaddeus Price first made his name as a deputy. Using only his bare fists and the sovereignty of his brass badge, he single-handedly rid Pointe Claire of a trio of drunken, malingering (there are those who alleged *inbred*) brothers who for years had terrorized every law-abiding citizen unfortunate enough to wander into the outer reaches of Ward Four. As their tarnished reputations flourished, the thuggish pranks of the Griffin brothers grew bolder. They began harassing the high school kids who came to park beside the moonlit banks of the Mississippi. No family outing or church picnic was spared their ruffian antics. Ward Four, at least those bucolic scenes beside the river, became a pirates' den.

Then Thaddeus Price joined the force. Deputy Price professed that if head-butting and bare-fisted brawling were the Griffin brothers' sport of choice, then that was good enough for him. He drove alone and unarmed out to the west bank of the Mississippi River, parked his cruiser and waited. When the Griffins showed their faces, as show them they must or forswear their truculent ways and retire from Ward Four, what took place was a three-ring free-for-all. Thaddeus beat them singly, in mixed pairs, and all three at once. He beat them standing, then he beat them to their knees. He beat their heads, he pulled their hair, he beat their limbs, he beat them everywhere. When one of the toughs fell prostrate, Thaddeus dragged him down to the edge of the river, revived him in the cool brown water and then beat him senseless again. This went on for an hour or so until the Griffins had enough. Then Thaddeus tied and trussed the three of them like wild game to the hood of his cruiser and drove through the parish for all the inhabitants to see. The Griffins were a nuisance no more.

Don't mess with Thaddeus became the cry of the land. Wherever mayhem or corruption arose, Thaddeus was sent to quell it.

The sheriff's office in Crossroads is on the first floor of the courthouse, around back. Sheriff Price is in attendance and seated behind his mammoth desk when I arrive.

"Come in, come in," he says, scrambling to his feet.

Standing there, the sheriff is one of the few persons I'm forced to look up to. He's not only big but tall—at least six-feet-seven by my guess, capable of playing havoc at either end of a basketball court. I would hate to try to keep him away from the backboard. Set free from the restraints of his police cruiser, he looks younger and less fretful. And handsome. I'm glad I opted for the silk blouse and wool slacks. The lace-up boots are back in town where they belong.

"Please sit down, sit down," he says, pointing to a vacant chair. "It's . . . Mrs. Morris, isn't it?"

"It's just Morris," I say. "Diane Morris."

"Please sit down, Miss Morris."

Sheriff Price resumes his seat and begins distractedly aligning the small piles of paper strewn across his desktop. Either he's forgotten what he's looking for or he has a nervous tic. He sees me watching and puts his oversized hands in his lap.

Do not open your big mouth. Let him start the conversation.

"Well," he says at last, "how can I be of help to you?"

"Oh, I just happened to be in the area this morning," I say, only slightly stretching the truth, "and I was curious if you've learned anything about the paint incident at Baughman's new horse barn?"

The sheriff seems somewhat relieved I've come calling on an official matter, something for which he can provide routine assistance.

"Not a thing," he says, shaking his head. "But I wouldn't read too much into this one occurrence. Baughman is not the most well-liked man in these parts."

"But you're not ruling out it was something more serious?"

"I'm not ruling out anything," he says.

The sheriff's tone is one of bland circumspection. I figure he's not telling me everything he knows. Or might suspect.

"Sheriff, yesterday at Baughman's barn, you mentioned some matter with Henry Dunn and a misunderstanding about a cow. Was it a stolen cow?"

Bingo. Sheriff Price's big hands move busily across the top of his desk again.

"Let's just say it's a question of law," he says.

"A cow was stolen?" I say.

"There was a cow," he says. "Its whereabouts uncertain."

"And presumed stolen?"

"Presumed missing," he says, avoiding my eyes.

"I don't follow, Sheriff."

Sheriff Price rubs the right side of his square jaw as if soothing a sore tooth.

"Amanda Snow agreed to sell a yearling to Baughman," he says. "She delivered the animal to Baughman's holding pen."

"So it was Baughman's cow," I say.

"It was in Baughman's pen," he says. "No money had changed hands."

"So Baughman was in possession of the cow although no legal consideration had been tendered."

"Yes," he says. "Baughman claimed he had merely agreed to buy the cow. Since no money had changed hands, no sale had been consummated."

"But there was the physical presence of the cow," I say. "Surely he didn't deny that?"

"Yes," the sheriff says. "When Baughman drove to the holding pen, the cow was gone."

"Stolen?"

"Missing," he says.

Sheriff Price absently pats his shirt pockets but comes up empty. I cannot tell if it's me or just the subject matter that makes him jumpy.

"I'm trying to understand, Sheriff."

As if enduring a complete dental breakdown, the sheriff now massages the opposite side of his jaw.

"When Baughman arrived at the holding pen," he says, "the gate was open and the cow was gone."

"The gate was left open?"

"Mrs. Snow claimed she personally shut and latched the gate. She had two witnesses."

"Someone had to open it," I say.

"We can rule out the cow," the sheriff says, his brown eyes twinkling.

The rules of the dialogue have now been established. I'm free to guess what might have happened and he'll keep me from going too far astray. It's like a game of twenty questions with flirtatious overtones.

"So," I say, "through the fault of a person or persons unknown, the gate was opened and the cow escaped."

"On that much we agree," he says.

"Was the cow detained or did it remain at large?"

"The cow was discovered the following morning in Henry Dunn's cornfield," he says.

"Then the case was resolved," I say. "The cow was found and returned to its rightful owner."

"The issue of who owned the cow was still under dispute," he says. "The cow was never returned."

"But Sheriff, you said the cow was found in Henry Dunn's cornfield."

"What was left of the cow."

"What *was* left of the cow?"

"Skin and bones," he says.

The sheriff's amusement has suddenly abated and his dental woes have migrated to his temples. He rubs his forehead with both hands.

"So," I say, "we now have a person or persons unknown wanted for possible cattle theft as well as its . . . untimely demise."

"The death of the cow was ruled to be natural," the sheriff says. "No foul play was detected."

"You said the cow was slaughtered."

"It was butchered," he says. "Henry Dunn claimed the cow died after he found it."

"So," I say, "Henry Dunn claimed he butchered a stray cow that wandered onto his property and died. Is there a law against that?"

"Not that I'm aware of," he says.

"What happened next?"

"Amanda Snow sued Baughman for breach of verbal contract. Baughman had Henry Dunn arrested for harboring stray cattle. The charges were later dropped."

"And Henry Dunn?"

"Dunn kept the butchered meat."

Sheriff Price turns in his swivel chair, aiming to rest one black-booted foot on the corner of the desk, then thinks better of it. He sits up straight and smiles.

"Sounds like there's no great love between Baughman and his neighbors," I say.

"The less interaction the better," he says.

The sheriff has been more forthcoming than I had hoped for. Either I play the nice girl and let him off the hook now or go for broke. I suddenly recall my cowardly supervisor's favorite edict: No guts, no glory. The man is afraid of his own shadow.

"Sheriff, do you suspect Amanda Snow or Henry Dunn may have removed their own boundary markers? Do you think it's in their interest to confuse the issue of existing boundary lines?"

The sheriff leans back in his chair and sighs, the weight of the world suddenly back in place.

"I'm not a lawyer, Miss Morris, and I cannot begin to predict how the issue of conflicting boundary lines is going to figure into this Mud Lake affair. But I can tell you this: Neither Snow nor Dunn is going to give up property without a fight. You can bet the bank on that."

"Then you believe one or both of them may be behind this barn-painting incident?"

"I wouldn't rule either of them out," he says. "On a short list of suspects, I'd put them near the top."

A uniformed deputy enters through a side door and stops dead in his tracks once discovering my presence. He stands wide-eyed, a slip of yellow paper grasped in one hand.

"Something I can do for you, Mitch?" the sheriff says, "Or do you figure on standing there all morning gawking at Miss Morris?"

"Sir?"

"You need to see me?" the sheriff says.

Mitch hands over the yellow slip of paper and slowly backs out of the room by the way he entered. He looks baffled, ambushed by an image not of his own making.

"Give us some warning next time you plan on stopping by the office," the sheriff says, "and I'll make sure Mitch is properly restrained."

I'm going to take that as a compliment and hold my tongue. Smile.

The sheriff carefully reads the yellow slip of paper, then tosses it atop one of the piles before him. When he looks up, he seems surprised to find me still sitting here.

"Tell me, Sheriff, what's the story with Amanda Snow? I spent the afternoon with her earlier this week but I got the feeling she was holding something back."

Once more the sheriff's brown-eyed gaze steals away

from me. His expression seems to rid itself of all emotion or intent.

"Did she mention her husband?" he says at last.

"She told me her husband had been killed. She didn't elaborate."

The sheriff retrieves a rubber band out of the cluttered top drawer of the desk and wraps it tightly round two of his fingers.

"And her daughter?" he asks.

"Amanda Snow had a daughter?"

"Has a daughter," he says, letting go the rubber band. "The girl and the husband were in a head-on collision with another car, on the road that runs in front of the Snows' house. The husband was killed instantly; the daughter has never regained consciousness. She's been in a coma ever since."

Coma. The word has its own hellish flavor. Dissolution of all human sense, all emotion. Alive in death, a breathing corpse.

"When did this happen?"

"Some time ago," he says. "Not long after I joined the department."

"Where's the daughter now?"

"Her condition requires round-the-clock care. She's in a home in Baton Rouge."

That explains much, accounting for Amanda Snow's largely self-imposed withdrawal from her own community. Grief, anguish, loss being the wellsprings of her character. If you rely on no one, you're less apt to be disappointed.

"How did Mrs. Snow take it?"

"She shut herself up in the hospital room with her daughter for almost a year after the accident," he says. "Her unharvested crops rotted where they stood; the bulk of her fields lay fallow. Friends of the family fed and looked after the livestock. Her whole place fell into ruin. When she finally returned to Pointe Claire her hair had gone from black to silver."

Sheriff Price consults the clock on the wall, then looks at his wristwatch. He bites his lower lip.

"There's more isn't there, Sheriff?" I say. "There's something else you're not telling me."

I can see the quick flick of contention in his brown eyes. He's deciding if he's going to tell me what he knows.

"There were circumstances surrounding the accident that went unexamined," he says. "It was a two-car collision on a country lane in broad daylight. The weather was not a factor. The driver of the other vehicle was under the employ of Baughman. One of his flunkeys with a history of drunken driving."

"Are you suggesting there was a cover-up?"

Now there is only something like anxiety in the sheriff's brown-eyed gaze.

"All that happened a long time ago," he says. "Under the watch of the former sheriff."

"Another of Baughman's henchmen?"

Sheriff Price leans forward in his chair and lowers his voice. His expression is kind, chivalrous.

"I offer you a free word of advice, Miss Morris," he says. "Baughman is used to having things go his way. Be careful how far you push him."

ten

After leaving the sheriff's office, I take a long drive down the levee road and try to clear my head. The morning sky is wall-to-wall blue, not a cloud or trace of haze to mar the vault of heaven. The wind blowing through the open car window is clean and cold. The brown, furrowed fields beside the levee await the arrival of spring—their promise of untold bounty to come.

My visit with Sheriff Price granted more information than I bargained for. It seems my trio of contesting landowners are separated not only by boundary lines but long-lived malice as well. Each of them seems perfectly capable of twisting events to serve his or her own ends. The further I delve into this Mud Lake business, the worse it gets.

It's evident the biggest obstacle to my achieving a boundary settlement is in the person of Baughman himself. Without his consent and cooperation, I have nothing. My task then is certain: I must bring Baughman into the fold somehow, make him see the wisdom of my proposal.

One way of accomplishing this might be by first obtaining the accord of his neighbors, isolating him from the others and thereby putting pressure on him and him alone. Raise the ante, as Pop says. With the approval of a boundary agreement by his neighbors in hand, Baughman will be outnumbered, making his position appear obstructionist and therefore less tenable. One against the many, his own obstinance working to my favor. Then I can begin to close the circle, see how he reacts to being squeezed. The stakes are high and this has gotten personal.

So my next move is not forward but lateral. Time to revisit Baughman's neighbors.

I did not always appear so glib and confident in the face of opposition. At the ripe age of twenty-three, near the end of my second week in the oil business, I was sent to Mississippi to obtain the signature of an absentee landowner named Priscilla Priest.

"Whatever it takes," my new supervisor chided me. "Just get that lease signed!"

Sixteen hours later I stood dumbstruck in the center of the living room of the Priest plantation home, my briefcase in hand, reluctant to move. In one of the two leather armchairs flanking an unlit fireplace lay a miniature chihuahua. The small dog sensed my uneasiness and growled, lifting one lip cruelly over its brown-stained teeth. I stepped to one side, almost knocking over a brass floor lamp, then sat in the vacant armchair.

I had managed to calm myself by the time Priscilla Priest crossed the foyer and stepped into the living room. In her mid-fifties, she was short and round as an oil barrel. Her arms hung down her sides like little Virginia hams.

"Mrs. Priest?" I ventured, setting my briefcase down and getting to my feet.

"My stars, Miss Morris, you're so young. And so tall!" she said, throwing her head back and hooting.

At the sound of her voice, the toy chihuahua jumped to its bantam feet, launching a major conniption. I hopped to one side, caught the falling brass floor lamp, and fell into the vacant armchair. With this, the chihuahua appeared to gain some measure of inward satisfaction, gave its genitals a robust tongue licking, then settled smugly back down on its haunches.

"What a lovely surprise, Miss Morris. So good of you to stop and call," Priscilla Priest said. "And what brings you here to Starkville?"

A little wave of yellow nausea splashed over my shoulders and landed at my feet. Had our telephone discussion of the day before regarding the oil lease slipped her mind? Now that we were face-to-face, was the woman playing hard to get? What the hell?

"The oil lease," I said, retrieving the documents from my briefcase and laying them on the coffee table. "The oil well in Assumption Parish. You said we had a deal. Don't you remember?"

"Oooh, oh yes!" Priscilla Priest said finally. "Yes, I do remember, Miss Morris. I do!"

The clammy sick tide receded. My dark premonitions were for nothing. Mrs. Priest would sign the lease and Anoco could drill its oil well. And I would keep my new job.

"But my stars, Miss Morris, it's not every day we are visited by the likes of Big Oil. We must celebrate. I won't be but a minute."

I sat quietly there in the living room, studying the hem of my new plaid skirt and the snoozing chihuahua. Never had I seen so many knickknacks crowded in one room. I was up on my feet, gliding across the floor before I knew it. On an end table beside a bookcase, I spied a small porcelain ballerina that stopped me dead in my tracks. She stood on tiptoe among a grouping of plaster Christmas elves, perfect, mesmerizing, like a virgin princess held hostage by savages. Even as I reached for her, I expected the ballerina to dance tauntingly out of my grasp. Instead, at the instant of my touch, the dancer's lean, uplifted leg snapped off cleanly like a stick.

Too stunned to flee, I jumped back from the end table and catapulted myself across the room into one of the plush leather armchairs. The horrible, sharp crack of the chihuahua's spine breaking under me made me retch.

The brisk, staccato footsteps of Priscilla Priest rang from the hall. I leapt to my feet, stashed the dead chihuahua and the ballerina's busted leg in my briefcase, then sat down in the armchair and tried to pull my skirt over my knees. I felt a slippage in time and space.

"Here we are, Miss Morris, some refreshments," Priscilla Priest said.

In her hands she bore a silver serving tray on which sat a cut-glass decanter and two tiny glasses. The sunlight pouring through the windows refracted off the tray and cut glass like magic. Small rainbows and bits of honey-colored jewels jumped across Priscilla Priest's face and hands.

"You look ill, Miss Morris," she said. "But a glass of peach brandy will fix you up."

She set the tray on the coffee table and poured out two portions of the thick liquor. Without pausing, she picked up one of the brandy glasses and tossed it off.

Suddenly I became calm, almost lucid. I realized my visit with Priscilla Priest hadn't gone as planned. If she learned the fate of her pet chihuahua, she might summon the police. Perhaps my future in the oil industry was kaput as well.

That's when it happened. That's when a little switch on the back side of my brain went *click*. Hadn't Priscilla Priest already approved of Anoco's lease terms? Hadn't all her brothers and sisters back in Louisiana already signed for their respective shares? Wasn't the drilling rig already on its way to Assumption Parish?

I picked up the typed oil lease off the coffee table and whipped out my black ballpoint pen.

"About this oil lease, Mrs. Priest."

"So rich and good," Priscilla Priest said, draining another glass.

Before she could pour herself a third drink, I set the oil lease on the coffee table, placed the pen into her stubby fingers and directed her where to sign.

"My glasses," Priscilla Priest said, laughing. "I should get my eyeglasses."

"No need for that, Ma'am. Just sign your name next to my finger. Now."

"Perhaps my husband should read this over?"

"Your whole family has signed this lease, Ma'am. Every lawyer in Assumption Parish has looked at it. Sign it."

"Oh, I suppose so. You seem such a nice young lady."

"They don't come any nicer, Ma'am. Please sign your name."

"Is there oil on my land, Miss Morris? Will we be tycoons?" she asked, then hooted.

"Millions of barrels of the stuff, Ma'am. *Sign* the lease."

And she did.

Wasting not an instant, I thanked Priscilla Priest for her hospitality, grabbed the executed lease and my overstuffed briefcase, then bolted for the front of the house.

"Do come again," she shouted from the living room.

"Always welcome. Always glad to see a friend. One for the road?"

I threw open the front door and strode out onto the sloping, green lawn. All around me sunlight fell in long, golden shafts. Overhead a flock of pigeons, like dirty-grey angels, hovered and dipped in the afternoon light. It was like a scene from an illustrated Bible.

Later, on my drive back to Baton Rouge, I stowed the dead chihuahua and the ballerina's busted leg in a roadside Dumpster outside McComb, Mississippi. It was a lonely stretch of road surrounded by dark, barren woods, and I felt as if I had crossed some kind of bizarre threshold, that there was no going back. But Priscilla Priest had her lease money and Anoco could drill its oil well and I would live to fight another day.

eleven

I ntuition tells me the best place to launch a breakthrough in my Pointe Claire boundary dispute is with
Henry Dunn, who is sitting alone on the front porch of his
irregular house shelling pecans when I pull into the yard.
In a fit of outraged possession, the yellow-backed yard dog
springs to his feet but is dismissed by a single word from
his master. Affecting an air of urgency, the mongrel ducks
under the house and yaps at the red rooster.

"Good morning, Mr. Dunn. Mind if I join you?"

"Come on up," he says.

Torn between the roles of cordial host and cautious
landowner, Henry Dunn half-rises from his chair and hand-
sweeps a few dry leaves from the seat of the wooden rocker
beside him. Thanking him, I sit down and select a few
pecans from the burlap bag placed between us. The pecans
are of the highly prized, thin-shelled variety renowned in
this part of the state. The shells crack apart easily in my
hand just by squeezing two pecans together. The sweetmeat
centers fall obligingly into my palm.

"Mr. Dunn, I've just come from the sheriff's office in town. Sheriff Price told me an interesting story about a cow. About a misplaced cow and an unlocked gate and a freezer full of butchered meat."

Henry Dunn smiles and nods his head, then runs his hand down into the burlap bag.

"The cow is dead," he says, "the meat's been eaten, and I don't know a thing about that gate."

"The cow was dead when you found it?"

"The cow was dead when I butchered it," he says.

Henry Dunn's expression might best be described as mischievous.

"How do you suppose it got out of Baughman's gate?"

"The cow?" he says, squinting.

"Yes, Sir."

Henry Dunn holds his empty left palm up for me to inspect. He then makes a fist and taps the back of it with two fingers of his right hand. When he opens his fist again, a thin-shelled, highly polished pecan sits in the center of it.

"I reckon the cow walked out the gate," he says, smiling.

"Amanda Snow claimed she locked the gate."

"I've been around cattle all my life," he says. "Never known one yet that could unlock a gate."

"Then someone must have opened it?"

"Other than the cow?" he says.

He closes his fist on the polished pecan, taps the back of his hand once and when he opens it, the pecan is gone.

"My guess is the gate was open," he says. "The cow walked out."

"Sheriff Price said there were no tracks leading from the holding pen. No tracks on the road, no tracks leading into your pasture."

Henry Dunn purses his lips and studies my words.

"Maybe the cow took flight," he says. "I don't know a thing about magic cows or how they move about. When I found the cow, it was near dead."

"But it wasn't your cow."

"It was in my pasture," he says. "Once it was dead, it didn't belong to nobody."

This being my second brush today with bovine metaphysics, I'm somewhat at a loss as to what to say next. Big Oil meets Alice in Wonderland.

"A cow appears mysteriously in your pasture and then drops over dead. Didn't that strike you as odd?"

"Good luck for me," he says, "bad luck for the cow."

Henry Dunn closes his empty fist again and taps it with a finger. When he opens it, the polished pecan is sitting there. He smiles, winks one eye, and then passes the pecan to me.

"You keep this handy," he says, "it's for luck."

I cannot help liking Henry Dunn. He comes across as someone capable of surviving, if not modestly prospering, in a land less than hospitable. I imagine as a younger man he was someone who might have moved about by night if necessary, with a swift eye, a quick hand. I wager he would do whatever it would take to benefit his kind and kin.

"I've been visiting with one of your neighbors, Mr. Dunn, about that Mud Lake business. Mr. Baughman is of the opinion all the lake bottom belongs to him."

"I suspect he is," says Henry Dunn, "but his opinion don't make it so."

"I agree with you, Mr. Dunn. What if I were to tell you Baughman is prepared to buy any land you own under the lake."

Henry Dunn's response is swift and to the point.

"What Mr. Baughman is prepared to do is Mr. Baughman's own private business. None of my land is for sale."

"I knew you were going to say that, Mr. Dunn, and I don't blame you. But if ownership to the lake bottom comes down to a legal fight, Baughman has many resources. Most of the local judiciary are in his back pocket. Getting something for the land might be better than getting nothing."

"The land is not for sale," he says. "That's my final word."

Henry Dunn collects a handful of broken pecan shells from the burlap bag and tosses them into the front yard. Misjudging the shells as a food offering, the watchful red rooster trots over and gives them a sound drumming with his beak.

"I was over at Baughman's place yesterday," I say. "Someone has left a calling card on the side of his new horse barn. A calculated threat, you could call it. Baughman led me to believe you and your sons might have had something to do with it."

Henry Dunn folds his long, thin arms into the center of his lap. He looks out toward the gravel road running along the front of his property.

"My Daddy," he says, "he came by train to Pointe Claire at the age of eighteen, riding in the back of a mail car. All the way from the state of Virginia. They put a piece of wire round his neck and tied his ticket to it. Like he was a piece of common freight. They fed him his dinner out of a old bucket. He stepped down from that train with nothing and nobody and not one welcome hand. Five years later he bought this property. Three years after that he had the land cleared and his first crop in the ground. He never asked for help and got none. It's now up to me and my boys to keep the place together. The land is not for sale. It won't be taken from us."

No funny business now. No sly rejoinders. No sleights of hand. Henry Dunn is prepared to fight for what belongs to him.

"Then let me ask you this, Mr. Dunn. If I were able to bring about a compromise where all parties—you, Amanda Snow, Baughman—agreed to divide the lake bottom along projected boundary lines, with everyone receiving his proportionate share, would you sign it?"

Henry Dunn's watery brown eyes flick away from mine and back out toward the road again. He rubs the raspy palms of his hands together as if warming them.

"I want what's rightfully mine," he says, "nothing more, nothing less."

It's our nature to want what's denied us. Should we ever acquire it, the difficulty is holding on to it. Which is worse: never to realize a burning bliss or to have known and then lost it? Where roams the father of my twelve-year-old son? How to allay the sorrow that binds my father's spirit? What I wouldn't give to soar to the basket's rim.

My teammates in college called me Sugar because I was all sweetness and light. I was, while it lasted, a bona fide idol. Once L.S.U.'s crowded Assembly Center cheered my every move. The student section rose to its collective feet and chanted my name. They stomped and screamed; they bellowed. Their clamor shook the dirt free from the rafters high above the gym floor; and every particle of dust that tumbled down had my name stamped upon it.

Sugar! Sugar! Sugar!

They called me Sugar because it pleased them to do so.

These days much of my time is spent driving through the open countryside. As I guide my vehicle past fields and sleepy villages, I am occasionally flooded with daydreams. I revisit the close games, the blocked shots, the sweet moves of my youth. I remember all of them. They come to me complete with tactile sounds: the squeak of rubber soles on polished wooden floors, the clamor of my name thundering off the gym ceiling, the pounding of my joyful heart.

Sugar takes the in-bounds pass at center court, breaks past a defender to the top of the key, head-fakes, then drives to the basket and lays it up and in. She scores! The student section erupts.

Sugar! Sugar! Sugar!

After leaving Henry Dunn's place, I drive down the levee road. Yellow sunlight streams through the windshield onto my lap and upon my leather purse lying beside me on the seat. Outside the winter morning is clear and brightly lit. A red-tailed hawk squats atop a telephone pole.

My best game ever, perhaps the single most intense moment of my life, came in the second half of the championship game against Tennessee in my junior year. I was in another zone. All the other players were wading in honey up to their waists and I was running scot-free. I moved with grace through, around and over the opposition. I *knew* where the ball was bouncing next; I *knew* which player was going to touch it. When a Tennessee player shot, I knew if she was going to make it before the ball left her hand. It was a game of ten flowing figures upon a white-lined court and I held the key. All sound, all meaning and motion were reduced to that one shining space and those nine other players. I was a grown woman sporting with girls. I scored twenty-eight points, pulled down twelve rebounds, blocked four shots. After it was over, my teammates carried me from the floor.

At the beginning of my senior year, sportswriters journeyed to Baton Rouge from across the South to watch me run unfettered up and down the court. They admired my rebounding, made mention of my speed and quickness, openly praised my poise and team leadership. I was described as a one-woman wrecking crew. Too bad about the early season injury. Too bad the human knee was such a complex piece of work. I remember sitting in my dorm room with my leg in a brace, peering at the color photographs and magazine articles and wondering what would happen next. The sportswriters had long since high-tailed it to other parts of the country where young women sat fidgeting, awaiting their turns in the spotlight.

For a year or so after Ray and I were married, I kept my collection of basketball trophies and memorabilia neatly arranged on a bookshelf in the living room. Dozens of gleaming trophies, some small, some tall, and all affixed with brass replicas of wavy-haired young women shooting jump shots. Eventually I put them away.

With two seconds remaining on the game clock, Sugar takes the in-bounds pass beneath the backboard, sidesteps a defender, pump-fakes, then tosses the ball through the hoop.
Sugar! Sugar! Sugar!

A bum knee is like a bad husband. Neither of them can be counted on in the clutch. After my knee operation, once I was freed from the awkward brace, nothing was the same. I lost three inches in my vertical leap. I was tentative, afraid to plant my right leg and push off. Even after moderate exercise, the knee would swell and require icing.

The word *betray* is defined variously: to deliver or expose to treachery; to disappoint the hopes or expectations of; to seduce and desert (a woman). Ray was a stubborn man guilty of many failings, betrayal being but one of them. He was also a wanderer, never happier than when sailing out the front door. At home he was morose and irascible, unable to sit still. Despite his protestations, he derived little pleasure from me or his green-eyed son. His favorite pastimes were all-night card games and drinking with his friends. He never washed a single dish. He had a knack for always disappearing when I was most dependent upon him. Our marriage was a persistent nightmare, like going up high for a rebound only to land and have one knee buckle under me.

twelve

I had not originally planned on visiting Amanda Snow
today, but with Henry Dunn's tacit approval of a boundary settlement in hand, I feel like pressing on. Mrs. Snow
is about to be seated for lunch when I knock on her
kitchen door.

"Come in this house and sit down," Amanda Snow says,
taking another plate from the shelf. "I hope you like turnip
greens because that's what we're having for lunch."

"That's very kind of you, Mrs. Snow, but I usually skip
lunch."

"Fiddlesticks," she says, stirring greens in a large pot. "A
girl skinny as you can't afford to miss a meal."

"Yes, Ma'am."

Amanda Snow hums a snatch of unrecognizable melody
while she bustles about the kitchen. She produces a second
place setting and a white linen napkin. Hot from the oven,
a pan of sliced cornbread is delivered to the table alongside a bowl of black-eyed peas. Tall glasses of iced tea complete the simple meal.

"Now pick up that fork of yours and eat, young lady," she says, taking her seat.

"Yes, Ma'am."

Accompanying lunch is my most despised daytime game show, broadcast into our midst by a portable television located atop the refrigerator. The program's contestants are being urged on by a studio audience as the former try to guess the retail prices of lavish consumer goods. Amanda Snow is not above voicing her own opinion should one of the competitors venture too far afield.

"That's a sterling silver tea service you're bidding on, sister, not a fry pan."

She laughs at the gullibility of the contestants and sprinkles vinegar on her greens.

"Have you heard the latest, Mrs. Snow? There's been some excitement over at Baughman's place."

"Excitement?" she says, distracted by the raucous bidding on the tea service. "What?"

"Someone painted a notice on Baughman's new horse barn. A warning for all to see."

Amanda Snow smiles and shakes her head.

"That's not what I hear," she says. "Some folks see it as an omen."

"Then you do know about it?"

"This is Pointe Claire Parish, honey. There are no secrets here."

The topic of Baughman's potential property woes seems to give Amanda Snow a small spasm of pleasure. Something like hilarity sparkles in her eyes.

"Yesterday I paid a visit to Baughman himself," I say. "He's of the opinion that Henry Dunn may have had something to do with those missing boundary markers. He implied Mr. Dunn was not above removing his own boundary markers if he thought it might help his cause somehow. He mentioned your name, too."

Avoiding my eyes, Amanda Snow carefully smears a pat of butter through the center of a wedge of hot cornbread, then sets it on her plate.

"Baughman's trouble," she says, "is that he can't get out from under the shadow of his Daddy. The old man's been dead for years and this one still can't find his way."

"You had no quarrel with the older Baughman?"

"Quarrel?" she says with quiet disbelief. "Nobody had a quarrel with old man Baughman because he didn't allow otherwise. You couldn't grind your sugarcane without dealing with the old man. Couldn't sell your cattle, gin your cotton. He paid you what he could afford to pay you and you were glad to get it. Glad somebody was willing to buy it. He was a ruthless old scoundrel, but he kept alive half the people in this parish. This boy of his is just a pale imitation."

"You don't sound like one of Junior's admirers?"

"He can rot in hell where he belongs," she says.

Amanda Snow's normally intense grey gaze blurs out of focus. Her fork lies idle on her plate. I reach across the table, touching her wrist.

"Sheriff Price told me about your daughter, Mrs. Snow. About the wreck and the circumstances surrounding it."

She removes her hand from under my fingers. Her next breath is one long hiss.

"They all lied," she says. "The authorities, Baughman, his hired hand, they all lied. The truth was never told."

There's no need for me to respond to these statements. My part is to be here in this moment and to bear witness.

"My girl lay in that hospital for nine days and nine nights," Amanda Snow says, eyes watering, "unable to even breathe without the aid of a machine. They fed her through tubes; they told me she was no more than a vegetable. They said she wouldn't live a week. But she wouldn't give up. She hasn't given up to this day."

Her speech is measured, deliberate, placing great store in its meaning. One wrong word from me might topple everything.

"I wish there was something I could say, Mrs. Snow, or do."

Amanda Snow reaches across the table and squeezes my hand.

"Don't you worry about me, honey," she says. "I have the farm here, my fields, my horses and cows. I spend every Sunday with my daughter. I don't have time to feel sorry for myself."

After clearing the table of our lunch dishes, Amanda Snow sets out cups and dessert plates, two silver forks. Dark-roast coffee drips in a blue enamel pot. On the television game show playing atop the refrigerator, bedlam has replaced all order. The studio audience has risen as one gesticulating body, driving the contestants to a leaping frenzy.

"Fresh pecan pie," Amanda Snow says, returning to the table. "I made it this morning."

She sets a slab of warm pecan pie and a fork square in front of me. Five thousand calories, I mentally calculate, five hundred laps around the block, two million sit-ups. And my very favorite.

"No," I say. "No, really, I shouldn't."

"Fiddlesticks," Amanda Snow says, trying to look past me to the television. "You come live with me a while and I'll put a little meat on those bones of yours."

Given the chance, I would do just that.

"Mrs. Snow," I say, standing and positioning my body between the older woman and the television. "Mrs. Snow, I visited with Henry Dunn this morning. He's agreed in principle to a boundary agreement concerning this Mud Lake business, provided everyone gets his fair share. If I were able to talk Baughman into agreeing to a settlement based on existing property lines, would you sign it?"

Amanda Snow laughs out loud and rolls her eyes.

"Honey," she says, "if you can get Baughman to agree to anything not to his immediate and sole advantage, you're a better trader than most."

"You let me worry about trading with Baughman," I say. "But you can help me by telling me what you know about this barn-painting incident. Do you suspect someone is trying to frighten Baughman? Flush him out of his hole?"

Amanda Snow lays her fork beside her pie plate and leans across the table.

"Honey," she says with slow conviction, "for fifty cents, I'd set that barn afire myself."

If you listen closely, most landowners will tell you everything. It is not uncommon for me to have only introduced myself, just settled into my assigned seat round the kitchen table, before they're telling me the intimate, sometimes lurid details of their private lives—things I have no need in knowing. It seems imperative I learn their husbands have just cheated on them or their unmarried daughters are pregnant or their wayward sons have taken up with dope smugglers. What business is it of mine which nephew is gay or whose ex-wife is sleeping with the Baptist minister? If Amanda Snow is aware of some harebrained scheme to terrorize Baughman by assaulting his property, why is she talking to me? How should I react to this news?

I once met a landowner who told me how he had burst into a locked bedroom only to find his wife hanging by the neck from a ceiling fan. The dead woman must have accidentally tripped the On switch when she kicked the stool out because the fan was spinning the body round and round in tight, ice skater-like circles in the air. The man said the sight of his heavily spinning spouse touched his imagination, and some minutes passed before he could bring himself to kill the small, overburdened fan motor.

A farmer once told me he had been struck seven times by lightning. The man said he had been forced to give up all outdoor work, that he couldn't find a job, that his family was terrified of him. He told me on one occasion all the hair on his body had been burned off. When he shook my hand, I was convinced I felt a little tingle of electricity.

In Lafourche Parish, I met a woman with six fingers on each hand who claimed to be a descendant of French royalty. She sat regally in her lawn chair while her husband served us hot tea in ornate china cups. I couldn't take my eyes off her many fingers.

To sit quietly beside a stranger and hear the ghoulish fate of a loved one or the telling of some bizarre personal anecdote are the types of encounters that do not leave a listener unscathed. These stories have a tendency to invade one's thinking, visit dreams, enliven memory, insisting they be told. I carry them with me wherever I go.

With unscheduled visits to Henry Dunn and Amanda Snow under my belt, I decide to drop by Baughman's place. I've got precious little to lose and everything to gain. And there's always the element of surprise.

Baughman's housekeeper greets me at the front door and escorts me through the house to the den. With the curtains drawn, the shadowy room emits a subterranean character, a feeble darkness that is neither day nor night; a fog-like gloom permeates my senses. The air is clammy cold, uncirculated. A spate of goose bumps crawls over the skin of my arms, up the back of my neck. The pervading silence is disturbed only by a faint clicking sound.

Stepping down to the sunken den floor into the anemic light, I can make out the massive shape of Baughman's recliner. Baughman's big head and rounded shoulders protrude above the chair's high back; his hideous, deformed feet lie crossed and reclined at eye level. I move cautiously through the murky air, sidestepping a coffee table, advancing slowly until I am positioned beside the bulky recliner. Anything seems possible: he might be dead, asleep, unconscious. The clicking noise is more pronounced.

"Careful of the dog," Baughman mumbles.

Crouched at my feet in the shadow of the recliner is the one-eyed dog. I take a step back, allowing a moment for my eyes to adjust to the gloom.

Baughman, in his pajamas, is eating a pork chop with his bare hands. Oily juices cover his chin and thick fingers. The clicking sound is the glancing of his teeth off the pearly porcine bone. He gnaws at the blackened chop with greasy lips and smacking tongue. Vexed by a stubborn shred of gristly flesh, Baughman opens his mouth wide and applies a great suck.

"If this is not convenient, Mr. Baughman, I can stop by another time."

Baughman gives the cleanly nibbled pork chop a keen

inspection, then reaches down and offers it to his dog. The animal takes the handout whole into its jaws and closes the one good eye greedily.

"What's on your mind, Miss?" he says.

Were it possible to isolate what I most dislike about this man, I might concentrate my energies to a point. It would be a beginning.

"I met with Henry Dunn and Amanda Snow this morning," I say. "They're both prepared to enter into a boundary agreement, provided everyone receives his fair share."

"His fair share?" Baughman says, frowning.

It's clear the concept of parity is foreign to him. Perhaps I can use his own greed to my benefit.

"Yes, Sir, inasmuch as you are the largest property owner bordering the lake, that leaves you with the lion's share of the lake bottom."

Using his index finger, Baughman draws a circle of clear grease on the armrest of the recliner.

"You are familiar with the concept of turf, are you not?" he says. "Even in the jungle streets of your cities, in the poorest of your bleak neighborhoods, there is some form of authority, a blinding will to order and possess, to dominate. Isn't that so? Mud Lake is part of my turf. I won't give it up."

"A court of law might see it differently."

Baughman dismisses my sally with a shake of his head.

"You will find no relief in the legal system," he says. "Not in this parish."

"I'm just trying to do my job."

"And so you are," he says, retrieving another pork chop from the platter on the coffee table. "You can tell my neighbors they're free to use the lake as they see fit. They want to catch themselves a fish, they want to sneak up and shoot a wild duck, they have my blessing. The lake bottom belongs to me."

"Then there's no chance of compromise?"

"It's never going to happen," he says.

"That might be an unpopular decision," I say.

Even in the dim light, I can see Baughman's pupils bulging in their sockets. He leans forward in the recliner.

"Listen carefully, Miss," he says. "There are bigger forces at play here than you can possibly imagine. You and your band of pesky locals are all expendable. I advise you to remember where you are and to behave accordingly. It could save you a lot of trouble."

In a perfect world, I would at this point produce a gilded saber and with it cleave the wagging head free from its body. But this is only business, and there is other game afoot.

"Then I can take that as your final word on the boundary settlement?" I say.

"You can take it any way you like, Miss," he says, his mouth filled with pig flesh.

"In that case, Mr. Baughman, I don't think we have anything further to discuss. Don't bother getting up, I'll find my own way out."

"No bother at all," he says, not moving.

Where is the end of it? Why am I forever being pitted against the biggest scoundrel in the land? Do I attract these types? Is it some perverse wish on my part to square off and do battle? Vanquish all. Or is it simply the luck of the draw?

Why can't I just let it go?

The levee road delivers me to the foot of the old Mississippi River bridge where I cross into Baton Rouge. From there I take the elevated expressway over the heart of the old city to Highland Road, which leads me south to the gates of L.S.U. and The Chimes bar and restaurant nearby. It is here, beneath the flag-draped ceiling of our former haunt, where I am to meet my wayward ex-husband, man of a thousand excuses, for a drink.

Why? Why see him, talk to him at all? Why put myself in such a position?

Because to avoid someone like Ray is a kind of cowardice. To hide from him is to risk giving him the upper hand. You don't deter a jackal by running.

The Chimes was the scene for much of the torrid romance between Ray and me. We sat in a dark booth in the back, staring inanely into one another's eyes and drinking an endless succession of imported beers. In the muted light, Ray's olive skin took on a blush, a sheen that was hot to the touch. Often, in the middle of a sentence, I forgot what I was saying; Ray would turn his bold glare in my direction, causing a disconnection between tongue and brain. I suffered from vertigo; my stomach did back flips. One minute I was seated happily in the booth next to him and the next I was tumbling into his moist black eyes. I couldn't keep my hands off him; more than once I pulled the hair from his chest. I wanted to milk him dry.

I park my car in back of the restaurant and, despite mixed emotions, run a brush through my hair.

"One drink and one drink only," I pledge. "Then we go our separate ways."

Gathering my coat and purse, I walk around to the front door of The Chimes. As if to confound my expectations,

Ray is on time and already seated in a booth near the front of the restaurant. He sits illuminated in a bolt of sunlight falling through a window high upon the wall, apparently lost in thought. As he is facing me, I can easily get his attention by waving or calling out, but I do neither; I just stand and look. It feels strange to see him again after a year and a half, and yet I am in no hurry to join him. Our last meeting ended in a public shouting match; I lost my temper and swore I would never speak to him again.

He looks older than I remember, heavier with less hair, a tortured look about the mouth and eyes, as if he were nourishing an exotic virus. The past few years have been hell for him. After his stint in federal prison, he took to fulltime gambling and all privations of the life that went with it. Contrary to everyone's advice, he marshaled the meager proceeds of his father's estate and opened a topless nightclub outside Biloxi. He was broke within a year. The last I heard he was managing a racetrack bar.

What happens to people? Where's the cocky young paladin I once walked with hand in hand along the shallow Gulf? Lit by the shaft of bright sunlight, his complexion looks pallid, a queasy expression about the gills. When the hostess asks if I'm meeting someone, I notice my palms are sweating.

"Diane," Ray says, getting to his feet, "great to see you."

He reaches to hug me but I swing wide of him and take a seat opposite in the booth. Long ago I imposed a *no touch* rule as far as Ray is concerned. It makes it easier to keep my focus.

"Yes, please sit down," he says, recovering his poise.

"Would you like a drink?" The light flashes in his soot-black eyes.

"A glass of water."

Something wet and cold, in case I need to douse him with it. Maybe this wasn't such a good idea.

Ray orders my water and a beer for himself from a passing waitress, then turns back to face me. The many fine lines under his eyes have softened his gaze, aged him.

"So," he says, grinning, "long time no see."

There was a period in my life when I would have walked on my hands to merit that smile. Gripped a rose in my teeth and done a hat dance. Begged.

"You said you wanted to talk to me, Ray."

He nods his head affably, as if fully anticipating my guarded reaction to our meeting face-to-face again. He puts on his kindest, most pliable expression.

"You've got every right to be annoyed with me," he says. "Every reason and every right. I've made a great mess of things, my life, our lives. No one knows that better than I."

Ray pauses here in his speech making, wetting his lips, weighing his options. Where's he going with this? Is he about to try something drastic, throw himself at my feet, crave mercy? He levels his black-eyed gaze to meet mine.

"You're still the most beautiful woman I have ever known."

"Stop."

"From the first time I kissed you, sitting in the back of this restaurant, I've been in love with you. I've been obsessed with you. And your big blue eyes and your perfect white flesh."

"Stop it, Ray. Stop it now or I'm going to leave."

The waitress arrives with the water and Ray's beer. She senses the discord seething in the booth and beats a hasty retreat.

"How's Tim?" he says, trying to lighten the mood.

"Tim's fine," I say. "He's young, happy. He wants to be an astronaut and fly to Mars. Why do you ask?"

"I'm his father."

"Who told you that?"

Ray recoils but doesn't lose his infamous cool.

"I know for now at least I'm the odd man out," he says. "A distant figure from the past. But my time will come. Sooner or later Tim's going to want to know his father."

"You took yourself out of the running as his father, Ray. You haven't spent a whole day with him since he was seven years old."

Pushed into a corner, Ray comes out swinging.

"Sooner or later he's going to want me back in his life. You wait and see."

"If you care about him at all," I say, "if his happiness means anything to you, you won't use him as a way of getting back at me."

Ray laughs and leans back in his seat. I notice for the first time he has begun combing his hair forward to mask a receding hairline. What else is he hoping to conceal?

"This is not about you, Diane," he says, swigging his beer. "I'm his father, he's my son. That's never going to change."

Ray is angling toward some resolution here, but he's not going to get any help from me.

"A toast then," he says, tapping his beer against the side of my water glass. "To what the future brings."

"This meeting was your idea, Ray. Why don't we cut to the chase?"

"There's my feisty girl," he says, grinning. "Always in a hurry, always hot to go. Your trouble, Diane, is you lack a sense of cunning. What I call gamesmanship."

"Unlike you?" I say. "Defender of the gambler's creed.

The willful diminution of everyone and everything before the high altar of what's good for you."

Ray doesn't so much as blink.

"I need your help, Diane."

"You bastard."

"There are some people following me," he says, looking over his shoulder. "People who will stop at nothing until they get what they want."

As I might have expected. Nothing short of a beating could have brought him back to Louisiana.

"It's about money, isn't it?"

"Among other things," he says, drinking from his beer. "There's been a little mix-up."

"You owe them money?"

"I've always paid my debts, Diane."

Ray becomes suddenly fixated with his green beer bottle. He scratches the damp label in half with his thumbnail, then shreds the remains. The indoor, sedentary life of the gambler has left his skin ashen.

"I need some time," he says finally. "If I could buy a little time, I could fix things."

"You must be desperate if you've come to me."

"Your father's got plenty of money," he says. "You could talk to him for me. It would be a loan."

The man's become a fool. It's almost too painful to watch.

"Dad wouldn't loan you a nickel if it meant saving your life, Ray."

"All I need is a stake," he says. "Just something to tide me over until I get back on top. I've had a bad run."

"A bad run," I say. "You've squandered everything a man might hope to have and now you call it a bad run? As if it were an errant hand of cards. As if some misalignment of the sun and planets were the cause of your problems. That losers, dupes and schemers are by necessity born under a bad sign. Do you believe that crap?"

Ray's not smiling now.

"You know me, Diane," he says, tilting forward in the booth. "I like being at the far edge of things. Seeing what's out there, pushing the limits. I wouldn't be happy living any other way."

This is the speech of one man failing: abdication of restraint and sole promotion of self.

"Then do it, Ray. March yourself back to Mississippi and do just that. Take up your life as riverboat gambler, regaler of young women, raconteur, and be happy. Or be miserable. It's your destiny. Only next time you belly flop, don't come crawling back to Baton Rouge."

Ray pushes away from the table now. Though he's getting beat about the head and shoulders, he has no choice but to play out the string.

"I live by my wits, Diane. I don't have a fancy college degree. I was never a star at anything, I was never part of the team. I didn't have your advantages."

"That's all bullshit, Ray. You're forty-three years old. I don't want to hear about your aimless childhood or your neurotic family. Get on with your life or shut up and live with the consequences. Or just shut up."

I reach into my purse, pull out a handful of cash and toss it in the center of the table. Call it insurance, call it a bribe, call it blackmail. Anything to get this squalling monkey off my back.

"It's not much but it's all I can afford," I say. "It'll get you out of town and down the road. Just go."

By the time I'm out of the booth and on my feet, the money has disappeared.

thirteen

Leaving The Chimes and the L.S.U. campus by way of Dalrymple Drive, I decide to take a spin around University Lake. The lake is a sprawling refuge set down in the heart of a garden city. Bikers, joggers, walkers and their pets move in detached harmony beneath the arching live oaks; bars of sunlight fall in brassy spangles across the shadowed lawns. The lake's unbroken flat surface reflects the cloudless winter sky so as to create a matching universe, cold and clear above, deep and blue below.

I cannot think of a better place to admire the big picture. Whenever I get bogged down in some phase of my life or work—a complex chain of title, a breakdown of negotiations in a critical trade, a conflict at home—I head straight for the lake, where I'm apt to remember no one is about to lose her life. That I am not solely responsible for the problem and some things are not meant to be fixed. That I am only one person. My role is to remain constant and open to any solution, to love my son and honor my father. All the rest I can offer up to the spirits of the lake.

Along the north shore beside the bike path, a refreshing breeze is always blowing.

When I pull into the driveway, I spot Crystal Haygood crouched beside an azalea bush in her side yard. From the looks of it, she has spent part of her day at the beauty parlor; the tint of her new coiffure is as vibrant as a blue jay's plumage.

"Good afternoon, Mrs. Haygood. You're looking lovely. Is everything all right?"

"Right as rain," she says, peering through the foliage. "Tomorrow is Friday, and I'm figuring on a pot roast. Slow cooked with potatoes and onions. What kind of vegetables does he like?"

"Ma'am?"

Crystal Haygood pats her indigo shock of hair and keeps a lookout for any sign of her quarry on my side of the azalea. Her undeviating pursuit of romance prevents life from ever turning dull; love is her one and only business.

"I haven't seen him since this morning," she says. "He's not ill, I hope."

"Oh, he's around somewhere," I say. "By the way, Mrs. Haygood, Pop and Tim loved the apple pie. They ate every last crumb."

"Every last crumb," she says, her eyes like two blinking fireflies in a field of bluebonnets. "Oh, my."

Crystal Haygood turns within her flowing kimono and glides across the lawn toward her back door. Woe to the man who thwarts her advances.

Tim is seated at the kitchen table when I enter the house through the garage. As described by his grandfather, my twelve-year-old son is the last of the hard chargers, by which he means Tim is forever on the attack and with everything he's got. Inquisitive by nature, Tim pursues mythology or algebra or the sports section with equal vigor. He looks up from his reading and frowns.

"You have a problem?" I ask, resting my hand on the nape of his neck.

"It's these gods, Mom," he says, squirming and holding up one of my old college mythology texts. "They act like a bunch of spoiled brats. How could anyone believe in them?"

"You're asking how the Greeks believed in their gods?"

"Who else?" he says.

Time for an audience. I set my shoulder bag and keys on the kitchen counter and join Tim at the table. He sits up straight in his chair, braced for action. His green eyes are big and wide. Out of some sense of fair play, he hands across the mythology book for my inspection. The book's yellowed pages are heavily underlined and the margins filled with cryptic notations in my handwriting. The passage he's been reading talks about how the Greeks made mankind the center of the universe, the most important thing in it.

Where's Pop when I need him?

"The author's describing how the Greeks saw themselves living in a world filled with terrific natural forces over which they had little control," I say, reading my old margin notes. "Their gods tempered this adverse relation between man and nature."

"So who was in charge of gravity?" Tim says, going on the offensive. "Where was the god of quasars? Or viruses?"

"I don't think that's the point," I say, skimming ahead in the text. "The point is the Greeks created their gods in the image of themselves, with arms and legs, hands and faces, emotions. Because their gods resembled themselves, the Greeks found the world easier to understand and less fearful. For the first time the world became a thing of beauty rather than something strange and frightening."

"What's so great about that?" he says, challenging me.

I'm not making much headway. Flipping a page in the mythology book, I find an illustration of bearded Zeus situated alongside one of the Egyptian gods, who is pictured as having a human body topped by a smiling cat's head. I place the open book on the table opposite Tim.

"Then tell me this," I say, refusing to concede. "It's a dark night and you find yourself alone, lost in a back alley. You hear something moving in the darkness behind you, and it's getting closer. So which of these two gods would you rather meet face-to-face? Sunny Zeus here, or this other character with the cat's head?"

"Zeus," he says without hesitation.

"I think that's what the author's getting at, Tim. The Greeks used gods made in their own image to describe the natural world and how it came to be, from the sun and stars to storms and earthquakes. Every bit of it."

Tim grimaces and stares at the open anthology. It takes him a moment to marshal his forces.

"But, Mom," he says, coming up for air. "How can someone believe in gods who sit around eating and drinking every day? And getting married and playing tricks on each other. How can you *believe* in that?"

Stalling for time, I pick up the anthology and turn to its introduction. In her opening paragraph, the book's author highlights the difference between the Old Testament conception of God and that of the Greek deities. Where the Hebrew God implied a harmonious, moral order, the Homeric gods assumed a world of random forces, morality being an invention of men. Tim sits quietly, awaiting my comments. The days of taking his mother's instruction at face value are sadly behind us.

"The author is saying Greek mythology is different from what we think of as religion today. She wants us to see mythology as a system of collective dreams, some of man's earliest attempts to explain the world without magic, without bowing down to gods with smiling cats' heads. She's saying the Greeks used poetry and stories, myths, to understand and explain the mysteries of life on this planet. The Greeks didn't believe the gods created the universe; they thought the universe gave birth to the gods."

Tim sits glaring, eyebrows furrowed in concentration. I've just hit him with a big roundhouse punch and he's still trying to get his feet back under him. But I know my son, and I know it's only a matter of time before he gets it.

"It'll come to you, Tim, just keep reading. It's nothing to worry about."

Tim leans back in his chair and breaks off his stare. He picks up the mythology book and flips back to the beginning. He reads.

"I'm not worried," he says finally. "I'm hungry."

"That I can take care of," I say, moving to the fridge. "By the way, where's Pop?"

"Pop said he wasn't cooking tonight," Tim says. "He said something about it being the blackest hour of the darkest day. What's that supposed to mean?"

The blackest hour. I'm an idiot. Thankless, self-centered daughter of a heartbroken man. How could I have forgotten?

"Today's the anniversary of your grandmother's death," I say, shutting the refrigerator door. "It slipped my mind.

You'll have to fix yourself something to eat. I need to talk to Pop."

My father has been part-parent, part-mentor since the beginning. A celebrated basketball player in his own right, Pop never revealed the slightest misgiving that his only child was born a female. On the contrary, he seemed to take particular satisfaction in my own athletic triumphs on the playing fields and ball courts. He worked with me every day, even if it was only a few minutes after supper. He taught me hitting, fielding, shooting, dribbling, passing . . . he taught me to anticipate my opponent's next move and how to beat her off the mark. Most of all, he taught me that beyond a certain level of physical prowess, all of sport, like life, was a contest taking place in the heart and mind of the individual competitor, and that the winner has first to best herself.

I find Pop lying flat on his back in his bed, his arms and legs draped over the sides. He peers up at the ceiling, inert, unseeing. Shackled and bound.

"Are you all right, Pop? Can I get you anything?"

"Nothing," he says. "I never thought it would come to this."

"You have to eat, Pop," I say, moving beside the bed. "A little soup? An egg? You have to keep going."

"Going?" he says, as if uttering the word for the first time in his life. "The earth has ceased turning, the moon has veered from its orbit."

It's this dramatic plunge into despair that always catches me by surprise. Somehow I must bring him back.

"That's not true, Pop. You have Tim and me. We have our life here, the three of us."

His sorrow is a knot of ropes binding him to the past.

"The trouble is I loved her too much," he says.

"She loved you, too, Pop. She loved every minute of her life. You know that."

His eyes still fixed on the ceiling, Pop lays his arms across his chest. His speech is slow, plaintive.

"In the weeks prior to her death, in the midst of her last treatments, weak, scarred, afraid, often too sick and full of poisons to sleep, she would wake me during the night. She spoke of her love for you and me, for Tim. She talked about her fear, her resignation, her faith. I never met anyone who loved life more than your mother. Anyone more generous of herself, her time. Anyone less deserving to die."

Were it possible to speak without choking up, I might describe how my mother's suffering touched each of us. Instead, I lie down beside Pop and stare at the ceiling. But my awkward silence is painful, too. Heartache may wander far and wide but often it huddles near.

"I've never met a perfect person," Pop says. "Your mother was not perfect, either. But she possessed brilliance. A brilliance of the heart and soul, a joy that fed the world."

The last time I saw my mother conscious she was awash with light. Somehow she had risen from her bed and was sitting erect in a ladder-backed chair before the window. An angular, white column of vibrant moonlight bathed her head and torso. Frail, hairless, hollow-eyed, her flesh and bones appeared almost translucent, the bright moonlight passing through her body as though it were mere paper. It occurred to me that my mother's corporeal self was slowly fading, slowing merging with the light. That soon she would be a part of that light. When she turned and saw me standing in the room, she fixed me with a look of such solemnity, such grandeur, that I was reticent to speak. She smiled thinly, nodded her head almost imperceptibly, then turned back to face the light.

"Whenever I have a difficult choice, Pop, a tough decision to make, I think of Mom. Would she approve, would she interpret the facts as I do? Will my solution be a step toward the light?"

Pop turns his absent gaze from the ceiling and looks at me, his grief contested by a smile.

"Your mother always hoped you would find a great love to share. That someday you would meet a man who felt the same as you."

I failed to see it coming but there it is: the eternal refrain. *Is Diane never to meet her dashing prince? Will the glass slipper never fit so that the two of them may steal into the night? What's wrong with young men today?*

"Don't start, Pop," I say, sitting up on the side of the bed. "Please."

"I just don't get it," he says. "You're a beautiful young woman."

"I live in this world, Pop. I have a job. I have a family, a house, hobbies. I have lots of friends, women *and* men."

"When was the last time you went on a date?"

"It's not always up to me," I say, jumping to my feet. My momentum almost carries me into the wall. I hate this!

"You might try making yourself more available," he says. "Get in the swing of things."

"I'm six-feet-fucking-four, Pop!" I shout, waving my arms in the air. "I'm thirty-three years old, divorced and a single parent. Men don't know how to deal with all of that. You understand? I'm not some young chick toying with her prospects. There *are* no prospects. None, zero. Are we clear on that?"

I might as well have slapped him across the face, flashed my tits. Pop shuts his eyes to avoid looking at me. His hot-tempered wench of a daughter. Now I'm to get the silent treatment.

"I'm sorry, Pop. I didn't mean to fly off the handle. OK? Do you hear?"

He hears me all right, but he's not budging.

"Look, Pop, you've got to stop thinking of me as just a taller version of Mother. I'm different. I have to find my own way, what's right for me. Do you see that? I'm doing the very best I can."

Pop gets to his feet and peers out the bedroom window into the night, keeping his back turned in my direction. He blows a puff of warm air fogging the windowpane, then rubs it with the heel of his palm.

"Maybe if I weren't always underfoot," he says, "you would have a better chance of meeting someone."

He's been holding back up to this point, but here come the big guns. Answer the question or duck and run.

"No," I say, moving beside him at the window. "No, that's not it. We're a family here, Pop. You, me and Tim. The three of us. Any man who cannot accept that has already taken himself out of the running."

"If I moved back home," he says, turning to face me, "it wouldn't be an issue."

There's one solution; now it's my turn. I straighten his rumpled shirt collar, then remove a long strand of blue hair from one shoulder. *Crystal Haygood!* What the hell happens around here while I'm at work?

"Listen, Pop. Listen to me carefully. I need you here, in this house. Tim needs you here, in this house. This is where you're supposed to be. This is where you're going to stay. Are we clear on that?"

Visibly relieved, Pop puts his arms around me and squeezes tight. We have this meeting of the minds every month or so. Like a good cry, it helps to clear the air.

"It's settled then," I say, kissing his cheek. "This is home. You're required to stay here until you get married again."

"What!"

If he didn't react so mightily to my teasing, it wouldn't be so much fun.

"When you get remarried," I say, "you and your new bride can fix up your own little love nest. Two women under one roof is one too many."

"Whoever gave you the idea I was thinking of getting married again?"

But I'm already out the door.

I restrict my nighttime reading to the den, where I'm less apt to remain awake to all hours than if I bring a book to bed. The den sits at the rear of the house, opening onto the brick patio and my father's most recent construction, a gurgling fountain and surrounding rock garden. With Tim and Pop secure in their rooms, the den area becomes my wistful hideaway—the site where I'm least likely to suffer intrusion.

So just when I think things have settled in for the night, Duke the dog sets up a sustained commotion in the backyard, and I'm not amused. Despite reaching the age of thirteen, our black Lab has ceded none of his self-imposed mandate to repel all interlopers, be they blue jay, stray cat, grey squirrel or butterfly. I open the sliding glass door and step out onto the patio.

"Hush, Duke. Hush now."

But having attracted an audience, Duke imbues his alarm with renewed fervor. Moving to the edge of the patio away from the glare of the floodlights, I perceive the motive of the dog's agitation. Backed up in the corner of the yard against the gate stands Duke's onetime master, Ray.

"Call him off, for Christ's sake! Son-of-a-bitch tried to bite me."

The prince of liars returns.

"My guests use the front door," I say, moving slowly toward the gate. "Why are you sneaking around the back?"

Ray's catalog of misdeeds has never included physical intimidation. Is this some new level of depravity?

"Just wanted to talk," Ray says, trying to make light of his predicament. "Can't you shut him up?"

I take hold of Duke's collar but keep him positioned between the two of us. One word from me and Ray is dog meat.

"Hush, Duke," I say, stroking his big black head. "It's all right now. Good boy."

"It's me, Duke," Ray says. "Don't you remember me, old buddy?"

Ray extends his open hand—the hand not holding the beer bottle—but succeeds only in raising Duke's hackles.

"OK, OK," he says, backing off.

"Why are you here, Ray?"

Not too drunk to feel the tenuousness of his situation, Ray pulls out all the stops. His tone is indignant, aggressive.

"I want to see Tim," he says. "I want to see my son."

"No," I say, not for one instant considering the request. "He's asleep."

"I'm his father, wake him up."

"No," I say. "It's late. You haven't talked to him in years. If Pop wakes and finds you here, he'll tear you apart."

Faced with the prospects of a charging grizzly for an ex-father-in-law or a lunging black Lab, Ray would fare better against the dog.

"Pop's here?" he says, retreating further into his corner.

"He's inside, asleep."

"For Christ's sake."

"I want you to leave, Ray. Now, this minute. You want to see Tim sometime, you call me. Call me ahead of time and we'll talk about it."

Ray sees the lay of the land all right, but he cannot stop himself. His pitch varies from assertive to fearful, his motives confused.

"The men following me mean business, Diane. These people are in the habit of getting what they want. I could use your help."

Sooner or later Ray is going to hit bottom and then maybe he'll try to pick up the pieces. Or he'll get lucky and win the lottery. Either way, I'm not going to be there.

"If you're beat, Ray, if you're finished, then it's time to quit. Just roll over and play dead. Go hide under a rock someplace. But do it quietly. And do it now."

Ray steps toward me, causing Duke to rear up on his hind legs, straining at his collar. Ray backs away, but old habits are hard to break.

"You could put me up for a few days," he says. "You owe me that much."

There's only one man in a million shameless enough to propose this gambit. It's a measure of his desperation.

"No," I say calmly, gratefully. "I don't owe you anything."

With no room to work his famous charms, Ray is reduced to flinging mementos.

"No one's ever loved you like me," he says, "no one's ever taken you so far, gotten so far inside. Don't tell me you forgot. Remember the moon in the trees? The nights along the Gulf? You can't throw all that away."

I remember all of that and much more, but I refuse to be bound by it. It occurs to me that I could end this fiasco by releasing my grip on Duke's collar. Let the two beasts go head to head. What's a girl to do?

"Everything you're offering, Ray, is what you've already taken from me. You've said what you came to say; now it's time to go. You pull something like this again, you show up here unannounced, uninvited, I'll put the dog on you. Don't think I won't."

I take Duke inside the house with me, lock the sliding door, pull the drapes and kill the light.

PART V

Friday

fourteen

6:30 A.M. The muffled explosion issuing from a back bedroom signals Tim's leaping, airborne dismount from his top bunk onto the wooden floor below. My gangly man-child has all the finesse of a sumo wrestler. Though shod (perpetually) in socks, his clomping footfalls echo like drumbeats down the hall to the kitchen.

"Good morning, Tim."

"What's for breakfast?" he says, barely awake.

"Let's try that again, Son. This time with more feeling."

"*Morning*, Mom. Can I have something to eat?"

"Come again."

Tim's uncombed hair is aimed in three contending directions this morning. It looks as if he went to bed wearing his bike helmet.

"May . . . I have . . . something . . . to eat . . . Mother dear?"

"Yes, my jewel. Only too happy to serve you."

Tim is not a morning person, but I see no reason to abandon all common courtesy simply because one of us has the blahs. I was awake most of the night myself. What little sleep I did manage was interrupted by a nightmare visitation from Ray. He had been the victim of a fiery accident and suffered horrible burns over much of his body; his ears, nose, lips and eyelids were particularly disfigured, looking as if they had melted and run together. Even more remarkable was my calm reaction to his defacement, how I felt so easily resigned to it, how its meaning seemed so abundantly clear. I felt pity for him, compassion, but no sorrow, no anguish, nothing like remorse. It was as if his cruel impairment discharged me from all obligations, past and future, leaving me free to pick up and go. At last I was done with him.

Not true. As far as Tim is concerned, I'll never be done with him.

"Tim," I say, fetching a cereal bowl and spoon, "your father was here last night."

"Here?" he says, turning in his seat.

"Yes," I say, placing the bowl and spoon on the table, "it was late, and he didn't stay long. He and I had words, then he left."

Tim turns back to the table and fills the bowl with cornflakes.

"Had words?" he says. "Explain."

"Your father and I seem to have trouble talking to each other. There are so many mixed emotions, bad feelings involved."

"What emotions?" he says.

Perhaps I shouldn't be burdening my son with this, but the time is coming when Tim will be forced to deal with his father. He may as well have some idea of what he's going up against, even if it's from my impaired point of view.

"Tim, I once loved your father very much," I say, sitting

at the table. "And I think . . . I know, in his own way, he loved me. But some bad things happened to him, to us, and afterward nothing was the same."

Tim sits frozen in his chair, his head lowered.

"What bad things?" he says.

How far do I want to go with this? How much is Tim prepared to hear?

"Your father broke the law; he stole money from some people. Later he broke some promises to me. Now I can't trust him. I can't trust him with my own feelings. I'm not sure I can trust him with yours."

Tim frowns and runs his hands through his hair.

"So why did he come here?"

"I don't know, Tim. He said he came to see you. But I wouldn't allow it."

"Why?"

It's not getting any easier. Perhaps it never will.

"Because I think your father may have been trying to use you to get something from me. Because I won't allow him to show up here in the middle of the night and turn our lives upside down again. If he wants to see you, spend some time with you, he'll have to make some arrangements ahead of time. He owes it to both of us. Can you understand that?"

Tim sits staring but does not speak. I move to the refrigerator and return with a glass and orange juice.

"What did he say after that?" he says finally.

I've got to give him something; he's twelve years old and deserves something.

"He said he wanted to see you but he didn't know how long he was going to be in town. He said in the future he thought the two of you might spend more time together. He said he thought that would be a good thing to do."

Tim puts both his hands on the cloth place mat and smooths the wrinkles flat.

"Did he say he would call?" he asks.

I retrieve the milk carton from the door of the refrigerator and set it on the table. I run my hand through his tangled mop.

"He didn't say, sweetie."

Tim fills his bowl to the rim with milk, overflowing cornflakes onto the table. Some things never change.

Like the passage of a savage winter storm, events of the bank hostage debacle have left me shaken and searching for answers. Save for the unmitigated violence, nothing was achieved and the human costs were horrendous—the hot blood of our citizens lay puddled in the downtown streets beneath the eye of the media's unflinching glare. No good was advanced: only the reinforced image of a brutal and feckless people broadcast to all corners of the globe. Except in this instance it was my people, my town. Our anguish.

In the aftermath of the standoff's bloody conclusion, the cameras turned their peering lenses to the circus of human intrigue. News teams were sent scampering to all corners of our state in pursuit of the usual suspects—practitioners of the ancient and the obscure, the one-armed French fiddler and the handlers of viperous snakes, avid consumers of garfish, alligator or fresh roadkill so long as it's battered and deep fried. A land of steamy bayous and parched flat fields, the haves and have nots, the absurd and the bewitched. The whole world sat and watched our fair state rendered once more as a picturesque region inhabited by a simple humanity, colorful, festive, ignorant, multi-tongued, racist, at once friendly yet bellicose, a fluke concurrence of the comic and grotesque, with eyes fixed inexorably to the past.

The media went looking but the subject stole away.

There's only one phone message waiting for me when I arrive at the office this morning. A. E. Baughman Jr. sounds as if he's run up six flights of stairs onto the roof and is about to jump.

"All hell's broke loose now, Miss!" he says. "I told you. Didn't I tell you? You gather up whoever it is you need to straighten out this lake bed business and get yourself up here. It's time."

Another bright winter morning, a day of high-flying, sun-speckled clouds. Traversing the wooden bridge above the Black Water Creek near the town of Crossroads, I notice the normally high water has retreated to its bed. Across the channel a dull crescent of yellow sandbar disrupts the lazy current. Shallow pools shimmer like puddles of blue ink.

Father, benefactor, man who taught me courage, devotion, purpose, guide me. Mother, watch over me.

When I arrive at Baughman's new horse barn, it looks as if a mid-winter carnival is under way. Half a dozen sheriff's vehicles, bright lights glaring, are parked crosswise in the gravel lane. A crush of local residents has gathered at the roadside, threatening at any second to surge across police lines. Uniformed deputies are struggling to keep the onlookers back a prescribed distance from the smoking barn, but it's like trying to corral fish in a tank. A volunteer fire truck is parked at the barn door.

Sheriff Price sits in his patrol car with the engine running, hands gripping the steering wheel. A clatter of contending voices blares from his radio; his flashing dashboard light paints one side of his handsome face a grisly blue. In the midst of the commotion, he appears an island unto himself.

"Morning, Sheriff. What's the trouble?"

"Fire," says the sheriff. "Fire's the trouble. As if I don't have enough to worry about."

"Any damage?"

"Water and smoke mostly," he says. "Mitch is working up a report."

"Any suspects?"

"For starters, I've got half the residents of Pointe Claire Parish," he says, gesturing to the crowd. "Take your pick."

"How's Baughman taking it?"

"Badly," says the sheriff.

As if on cue, Mitch the deputy trots up, notebook in hand. He sees me standing beside the sheriff's car and stops dead in his tracks, struck dumb once more. Mitch is blue-eyed and hatless with thin blond hair shaved so close to his scalp he looks bald. His starched uniform crackles when he moves.

"Your report, Mitch," says the sheriff. "You do have a report?"

"Yes, Sir," says Mitch, recovering his bearings. "No doubt about this one, Sheriff. We've got a class II felony arson on our hands. Presence and use of flammables detected. Flash point location is positive. Primary ignition is put at 4:00 A.M."

"Give it to me in plain English, Mitch," says the sheriff, staring at the smoking barn.

"Someone gathered up a big bunch of paper and lum-

ber scraps in the center of the barn floor and set it afire,"
says Mitch. "Looks like they used diesel or gasoline to light
it. I'd say early this morning, several hours before day-
break."

Sheriff Price's body appears to visibly sag on its powerful frame. He takes a deep breath, then lets it go.

"You think they meant to burn the thing down or were
they just making some kind of statement?" asks the sheriff.

Mitch touches the short blond spikes atop his flat head
and mulls the question.

"You might be right, Sheriff, you might be right," he
says, "but I'd say one more statement like this one will be
the last one. If you ask me—"

"That'll do, Mitch," says the sheriff. "Go clear some of
those folks away from that fire truck."

"I tell you what gets me, Sheriff, what gets me is the
way—"

"Just do what I said, Mitch. Will you do that?"

"Yes, Sir."

The sheriff pops a chalky antacid tablet into his mouth
and grinds it to a powder before swallowing.

"You think there's a connection between the fire and
this Mud Lake business, Sheriff?" I ask, moving alongside
the patrol car's lowered window. "You think someone is
making good on Wednesday's warning?"

With the flat of his hand, the sheriff wipes a thin layer of
dust off the dashboard, then brushes the leg of his pants.
His big brown eyes scan the crowd.

"That's one possibility," he says, nodding his curly black
head of hair. "Or it might be a copycat crime. Once this
kind of behavior gets started, it's hard to put a stop to it."

"Any witnesses?"

"Nobody's seen a thing," he says, grimacing. "I've got two hundred people with nothing better to do than spend all morning watching a barn smoke, but nobody's seen, nobody knows a thing."

"No harm to the horses?" I say.

"None whatsoever," he says. "All the horses are still up at the old barn. The arsonists would have known that, of course. If they had wanted to start a real fire, do some real mischief, they could have set one there. I figure this little production was all for Baughman's benefit. Let him get a taste of what *might* happen."

The sheriff taps the steering wheel with both hands, his inner agitation making outer display. The muscles running along his tanned forearms ripple and flex.

"You see that crowd standing by the road there, Miss Morris?"

"It's Diane."

The sheriff reaches to remove his cowboy hat but finds it already lying on the seat beside him. His likable face splits into a goofy grin. Quickly he regains his composure.

"You see that crowd," he repeats.

"I see it, Sheriff."

"In that entire crowd of people," he says, "friends and neighbors, good citizens every one, there's not a single man, woman or child who wouldn't mind seeing Baughman get what's coming to him. Not one among them who, if he thought he had a fair chance of getting away with it, wouldn't strike the match that set this morning's fire."

"Sounds like you've got your work cut out for you, Sheriff."

He sits musing at the wheel of his cruiser, grimly detached from all the surrounding hoopla. The knight-errant surveys the field.

He reminds me of a man in need of bonny comforts.

Henry Dunn and his three sons stand at the roadside watching the smoke billow from Baughman's barn door. When he sees me approaching, he starts to doff his hat but changes his mind and simply nods and waves his cane.

"Morning, Mr. Dunn," I say. "Nothing like a little excitement to gather a crowd, is there?"

"A good fire is a sight to behold," he says.

"Only thing wrong with this one," says Lester, "is not *enough* fire."

"You got that right," says Zach. "What we need is less smoke and more fire."

"And some crackling tall flames," says Eugene. "I like a hot fire."

"And a cold glass of beer," says Lester.

"That'll do," says Henry Dunn.

The Dunn brothers, a bustling trio of high-fives and backslaps and expansive merriment, form a circle off the side of the road among the milling crowd. The whole assembly breaks into raucous laughter when one of the volunteer firefighters accidentally turns his high-pressure hose on a comrade, sending the latter cartwheeling across the gravel drive into the side of the barn. In the resulting confusion, the bucking, backlashing hose gets free, pummeling the entire fire company before being brought under control.

Henry Dunn stands alone and seemingly preoccupied, immune to all the jubilation.

"I just spoke to the sheriff, Mr. Dunn; he thinks there's a connection between the fire and this Mud Lake business.

That somebody might be following through on the painted warning."

I've never been accused of faintheartedness, but this may have sounded a bit blunt. Sometimes I get ahead of myself.

Henry Dunn turns and looks me straight in the eye.

"There's no telling what some folks will do when they get pushed into a corner," he says, adjusting the brim of his hat. "I saw my Daddy once back down a posse of night-riding drunks with nothing but his cane knife. He told the men they might sure enough hang him in a tall oak tree, but not before one or two of them lost their heads. He asked them to point out the first one that was going to climb down from his horse and put a hand on him. *Point him out to me,* he told the mob, *let me look into the face of that man.* They finished their drinking and talking and rode on home after that."

Of the several stories I've heard about his father, this last one seems to give Henry Dunn the most pleasure. He stands up straight, his eyes fixed on the smoking barn.

"The sheriff says Baughman is quite beside himself," I say, "that there may be hell to pay for this fire business. I guess that's to be expected."

My observation is met with calm assent by Henry Dunn.

"I expect Mr. Baughman is not his usual self this morning," he says, watching the clouds of reeling smoke drift skyward. "Fire takes its toll on a man."

Beside the pumper truck across the way, a squad of firemen is rolling a length of hose into a giant coil beneath the critical eye of the crowd.

"You boys be careful now," calls one mocking onlooker. "Watch it! Ain't but six of you and one piece of deadly fire hose."

"Look over there, Alice," cries another wit. "It's Benny Gilbeau all dressed up like a real fireman. Hey, Benny! What did you give for that yellow hat?"

Amanda Snow stands at the roadside staring intently toward the smoking barn, her hands buried deep in the pockets of her red jacket. Her stance is critical, imposing, resembling a tiny, white-haired general overseeing the bombardment of the enemy camp. Wonder if she's packing her pistol?

"Good morning, Mrs. Snow. Looks like everyone in Pointe Claire has quit farming and taken up fire watching."

"Honey," she says, hugging me around the waist. "I wouldn't miss this for anything."

"Sheriff Price thinks someone might be trying to force Baughman into settling the Mud Lake business," I say.

Her eyes flicker as bright as Christmas lights.

"It will be good for him," she says. "Teach him not to put so much stock in the things of this world. You know what they say, honey, ashes to ashes."

Amanda Snow cocks her head and smiles broadly.

"Besides," she says, "it's only a small fire. Next time he might not be so lucky."

"Have you seen anything of Baughman?" I ask.

"He came glaring by here a while ago, but he doesn't want to talk to me," she says. "He's nothing but a yellow coward. That's the first thing you notice about a bully, that underneath he's all talk. He's been that way all his life."

"You sound like you feel sorry for him?"

"Not sorry," she says, shaking her head. "Pity. A mama's boy who grew up in the long shadow of his father. He thinks the rest of us can't see his fear when it's all there is to see. The more he tries to hide it, the more it shows. He gets more pitiful every day."

Amanda Snow shuts her steel-grey eyes a moment as if dispelling a bad memory. When she opens them, I become certain of my next move.

"Excuse me a minute, Mrs. Snow, I need to have a word with Baughman."

"Take your time, honey, wild horses couldn't drag me away from here."

People are like snowflakes, no two the same. That's what makes my job so fascinating. I never know what kind of person I'm going to run up against next: failure, survivor, pariah, savant, village idiot, craven villain or local hero. This latter breed, the native heroes, come in all shapes, sizes and colors, and are more numerous than one might suspect. Henry Dunn and his father spring immediately to mind, as well as the indomitable Amanda Snow. Champions, by my estimation, not necessarily by daring deed or bloody encounter but by how they conduct themselves every day. Men and women living lives of quiet distinction. What they do, what they value, being unopposed to who they are.

Baughman is leaning over with his giant head thrust partway into the sheriff's patrol car. His face is smudged with ashes and his clothes are filthy.

"I don't give a goddamn what the law says, you hear?

They're trying to burn me out. It's blackmail, I tell you! Blackmail and criminal mischief. I want it stopped. I want it stopped today."

Sheriff Price puts his huge hand in the center of Baughman's chest and gently pushes him away from the open car window.

"Calm down a second," says the sheriff. "I can't start arresting people just on your say-so."

"Why the hell not?" says Baughman. "Do you have to walk in on them setting the place afire? Catch them striking matches and spilling diesel?"

"I need some kind of physical evidence," says the sheriff. "And a motive."

"Motive!" says Baughman, advancing back to the patrol car's open window. "The motive is to cheat me out of what's mine. The motive is robbery!"

Baughman's frenzy stands in odd relation to the sheriff's pained consternation. The latter seems strangely subdued, as if he is hoping to avoid a scene. Baughman, meanwhile, waves his short arms in the air, gnashing his teeth, his eyeballs blazing. A near perfect imitation of a man suffering with rabies.

"Like it or not," says the sheriff, "I can't throw up a barricade around this one isolated horse barn. I've got six deputies and eight hundred miles of highway and country roads to patrol. Whoever we're dealing with here has got time on their side."

"Sounds like the criminals are running the show here," Baughman shouts, rapping the top of the sheriff's vehicle with his open hand.

Unaccustomed to having his cruiser used as a sounding board, the sheriff visibly flinches.

"Whoever did this," he says calmly, "whoever is responsible can come back to finish the job whenever they wish. Next week, next month, next year."

"What are you trying to tell me?" says Baughman.

Sheriff Price lowers the volume of his police radio and rubs the back of his neck.

"I'm saying if it was me, if it was my new barn sitting out here in the middle of the godforsaken woods, I'd think about meeting my neighbors halfway."

Baughman's head is back in the open car window now, his face flushed with blood and twisted in malice.

"Since when did you join up with that pack of thieves?" he shouts. "Give up part of the lake bottom? That's your advice?"

Gently, Sheriff Price backs Baughman away from the car window.

"It's a lot cheaper than building a new barn," says the sheriff.

"Where's it going to end?" cries Baughman. "If I give in now, what's to stop them? Next they'll set fire to my fields, run off my livestock and burn down my house!"

The sheriff pops another antacid tablet into his mouth and shuts his tired eyes.

"Take my word for it," he says finally, "you settle this lake bottom situation and your barn problems are over. I can almost guarantee it."

Baughman staggers back away from the patrol car and turns to face me. His expression is hysterical and his eyeballs are big as duck eggs.

"You might think of it as a business matter, Mr. Baughman," I say. "The cost of doing business."

Baughman raises his right arm as if to throw a punch at me but, perhaps realizing the proximity of the sheriff, decides against it. A real pity—if he so much as touches

me, I'll deck him. Baughman lowers his arm, jams both
fists into his pants pockets and kicks at the dirt between us.
He's backed all the way into a corner now, and how he
reacts to it will depend entirely upon his character. I like
my chances.

"You've got that boundary agreement worked up?" he
says.

"It's in my car."

"Get it, Miss."

⁂

I retrieve the boundary agreement from its file in my
briefcase, round up Henry Dunn and Amanda Snow, and
rejoin Baughman beside the sheriff's idling patrol car.
After reading aloud the typed, three-page document, pausing to decipher several of the more obtuse clauses, I offer
the agreement for general inspection.

"Any questions?" I ask.

Amanda Snow steps into the center of our circle of concerned citizens and points her finger at me.

"All this gobbledygook comes down to exactly what?"
she says. "Tell us what it means."

The deal has taken on a magical flight of its own now.
All I have to do is move slowly, carefully, and avoid flaring
anyone.

"It means everyone gets his fair share," I say, "based on
how much of his property borders on the shore of Mud
Lake. Mr. Baughman receives the biggest portion of the
lake bottom because he owns more of the shoreline."

"That was his Daddy's doing," says Amanda Snow. "This
one didn't have a thing to do with it."

Baughman groans audibly but does not counter her salvo.

"Regardless of acquisition," I say, stepping in, "the property belongs to Mr. Baughman now."

"Owning it is one thing," says Amanda Snow. "Deserving it is another."

I shoot an unheeded warning glance in her direction. We've come too far to get bogged down in polemics.

"How about you, Mr. Dunn," I say. "Do you have any questions?"

The untainted morning sun lends an alluring copper sheen to Henry Dunn's face and hands.

"This paper says my share of the lake bottom is mine," he says. "Everything on it and under it is *mine*. All of it."

"Yes, Sir," I say. "You own all the land, the minerals, and all the legal rights associated therein."

"Any fish I happen to catch belongs to me," he says. "I kill a duck, he's mine."

"Anything you kill or catch on your property is yours," I say.

Henry Dunn looks off at the smoking barn door as if consulting an oracle.

"Just like that missing cow," he says after a minute.

As if struck by the same willow switch, Amanda Snow and Baughman turn in unison and glare at Henry Dunn.

"That's a whole different story," I say, hoping to avoid a melee. "A different story with a different set of facts."

"That's another fine mess you people have made me suffer through," says Baughman.

"Oh, shut up, you big baby," says Amanda Snow. "It was *my* cow to begin with."

"OK, folks," I say. "Let's get back to the business at hand. We all seem to be in agreement about the lake bottom. Everyone gets his fair share, everyone's happy."

I lay the boundary agreement on the hood of the sheriff's cruiser and flip over to the signature page. I produce a pen and remove its cap.

"So who wants to sign first?" I say, my pen extended.

No takers. I might as well be offering them a rattlesnake to hold.

"Who's first?" I repeat. "Once this agreement is signed and sealed, Anoco can drill its oil well. Then there will be plenty for everyone."

All my landowners have suddenly become entranced with their own feet. Something has got to give.

"How about you, Mrs. Snow?" I say. "Ladies first? I need one of you to get the ball rolling."

Amanda Snow pulls the collar of her red coat up tight around her neck. Her grey eyes burrow into mine.

"Is this the best deal we're going to get?" she says. "Is that what you're saying?"

This is the axis about which all trades sink or flourish, the place we've been circling for days.

"It's not only the best deal, Mrs. Snow, it's the only deal," I say. "You going to have to trust me on that."

Amanda Snow takes my pen and executes the boundary agreement right there on the hood of the patrol car.

"Signed, sealed and delivered," she says, returning my pen. "I'm taking you at your word, honey."

As Baughman has become suddenly engrossed with the soiled sleeve of his white shirt, I turn to Henry Dunn.

"Would you do me the honor, Mr. Dunn?"

As if concluding a long deliberation within himself, Henry Dunn stands motionless, then blinks his bright eyes twice. He shifts his silver-headed cane from his right hand to his left and grasps the proffered pen. He moves to the hood of the patrol car.

"Don't mind if I do," he says.

Henry Dunn executes the document with a slow, ornate and sweeping signature that nearly runs off the edge of the page. Beneath his sprawling name he adds a kind of arabesque design that resembles an oil derrick.

"Give me that pen," says Baughman, snatching the instrument out of Henry Dunn's hands.

Baughman's hasty autograph looks like the Greek letter ξ.

"Are we done now, Miss?" he says, tossing my good pen onto the cruiser's hood.

As a further precaution, and just to see how close I can push Baughman to the brink, I instruct each of the signatories to initial the attached plat which depicts Mud Lake at approximate high water, the underlying premise of the compromise. After completing this task, I ask each of them to initial all pages of the agreement.

"Is all this really necessary?" asks Baughman, about to blow.

"Just so there's no misunderstanding," I say.

Once each of them has initialed the plat and all pages, I sign as one witness and pass the papers through the driver's side window for the sheriff to act as the other.

"Sign here?" the sheriff asks, giving me a sly wink.

"Yes, Sheriff, right below where I signed."

Though it took some doing, I've managed to stretch a thirty-second transaction into a ten-minute ordeal, at least for one of the participants. One must take pleasure where one can find it.

"After you record that document," says Baughman, "I'd like to have a copy."

"I'll personally drop a copy off at your house," I say.

"Don't bother, Miss," he says, shaking his ugly head.

"You just go on back where you came from and mail it to me."

Ignoring his fellow landowners, Baughman looks over toward the crowd milling in front of the horse barn.

"Sheriff," he says, "now that we've finished our business here, how's about clearing these people off what's left of my property?"

fifteen

After leaving the chaotic scene at Baughman's new horse barn, I pick up the river road heading south. The best part of my job is the long drives in the country, the time spent riding up and down the rural highways connecting Baton Rouge with surrounding towns and villages. It's not uncommon for me to drive an hour or two to spend fifteen minutes visiting with a landowner about his property or some minor question concerning his lease. Our business concluded, it's back down the two-lane highway for home.

There was a point in my career when I forced myself to listen to music and recorded books while driving—my thinking being that I was remiss in not taking advantage of all this dead time at my disposal. But after some months of concerted listening, I decided it was mainly a distraction keeping me from a deeper understanding, a deeper communion. These days I just ride in silence and try to stay focused on the here and now. I pay close attention to wildlife and the passing countryside, the play of sunlight and shadow across the open fields and spaces, the changing seasons.

There is a great comfort, a quiet gathering of oneself that comes from all these years of driving alone. Sometimes I feel as if I'm slowly filtering down through layers of cluttered anxiety to some sure center of myself. If nothing else, I've learned not to fret about life as much as I once did. I've discovered that regardless of what kind of load I might be carrying, I can still set it aside, still give it a rest. I've learned that worry is a substitute for action.

Today the gods are smiling.

My all-time favorite drive is the winding blacktop road along the Mississippi. One of the locked gates granting access to the levee and the river beyond is open and unattended. Public access to the Mississippi is normally restricted to the infrequent ferryboat landings so whenever I have the chance to gain a closer look at the river, I take it. Often the resulting view is spectacular.

I drive up the levee's steep incline to the top and step out of my car. From this vantage point I can see for miles, upriver and down, as well as across the wide expanse of channel to the far shore. With the general lack of heavy rain these past few weeks and the clear overhead sky, this morning the river is dirty-blue. A churning, roiling, titanic wall of water resembling an inland lake, only it's moving, rising out of the north and surging south. Upon its broad back are borne all manner of pleasure and commercial traffic; along its rugged banks roam deer and turkey and the last of the black bear and, according to some landowners I've met, a few lone wolves. Even as I stand here overlooking its passing, I have difficulty getting my mind around something on this grand a scale, a colossal barrier sundering the land east from west, sectioning the ancient wilds from the city streets—a raging, immense, watery deity, managed to some degree but forever unfaithful, untamed and intractable.

Like some men I know.

Between the base of the levee and the river's edge stands a leafless, russet-brown forest of willow and cottonwood trees. Idling in the calm backwater near the shoreline, a small red-and-white tugboat is in the process of securing a raft of empty barges to a stand of willows at the river's edge. Suddenly the tug sounds a tremendous blast of its foghorn that fills the woods and sky, resonating through my very bones. On the heels of this blaring fanfare, the tug's captain emerges from the control tower and fixes me in his binoculars. After a minute or so he lowers the glasses, pumping both his arms high over his head, and I, feeling pretty damn spry myself this morning, wave broadly back. He reenters the control tower and sounds his horn again: three splendid blasts.

All in a day's work.

Had I not been so enamored with my friendly tugboat captain, I might have noticed the flashing lights of Thad Price's vehicle pulling up the levee. The slow-rolling cruiser comes to a full stop behind my parked car and out steps the high sheriff. He strolls over to where I'm standing, taking his own sweet time.

"Hello again," I say.

Thad Price is all long limbs and playful smiles. He removes his white cowboy hat and knocks it against his thigh.

"Miss Morris, I'm thinking of assigning a full-time deputy just to keep a line on your whereabouts," he says, still smiling.

"That's very flattering, Sheriff, but unnecessary. My business is finished here. I'm on my way back to town."

"But you do get around," he says, "I have to hand it to you. When not attending barn burnings or stirring up the locals, you're trespassing on private lands. I may have to run you in."

"Now, Sheriff," I say, matching his jocular tone. "You know as well as I that gate was already open when I got here. I just drove up the levee to see the river."

"Another unlatched gate," he says. "What next?"

The sheriff looks out toward the river and runs his fingers around the crown of his white hat.

"Mighty fine view, isn't it?" he says.

"It's magnificent."

A stiff west wind creates a slight chop on the river's surface, reflecting sunlight in countless liquid mirrors. A convoy of low-flying wild ducks barrels down the main channel and out across the way.

"I grew up on this river," he says. "Hunting, fishing. When I was fifteen, two of my friends and I built a pontoon raft and floated down to Baton Rouge. They put us on the six o'clock news."

He looks across the sunlit channel to the flat horizon, then back to me.

"Tell me, Sheriff," I say. "What's it like out there? What's it like out there in the big middle of it? Tell me."

The sheriff's brown eyes search my face for signs of jest or sarcasm. Then he grins.

"It's like nothing you can compare," he says. "Like standing at the rim of the Grand Canyon. Or the top of the Great Divide. There aren't many places like it. Not around here anyway."

"Is it safe?"

"Safe?" he says.

"On the river," I say. "Is it a safe place to be?"

The sheriff dons his cowboy hat and pats one of his shirt pockets.

"You have to respect the river," he says, nodding his head. "Treat it with a healthy dose of respect, but it's nothing to fear."

Down at the river's edge, the red-and-white tugboat finishes tying off its raft of empty barges and backs away from the shore. Once reaching the deep water, it turns down river for Baton Rouge. Sheriff Price clears his throat and turns to face me.

"Just so happens I own a boat, Miss Morris."

"It's Diane."

"Yes," he says, nodding. "I know . . ."

"You were saying, Sheriff?"

He removes his hat and studies the headband as if a list of his intentions were written there.

"If you were interested," he says casually, "if it was something you might like to do, I could take you for a ride on the river one day. If you really want to see it."

"A boat ride?" I say.

"If you liked," he says.

As if anticipating a guarded response on my part, the sheriff begins shaking his head from side to side; his bold invitation has surprised us both. With the ball placed squarely in my court, this is no time for coy comebacks.

"A ride down the river sounds like a lot of fun, Sheriff. How big is this boat of yours?"

"Plenty big," he says, laughing and gesturing with his long arms. "Plenty big enough. Don't you worry about that."

I have an inkling a woman wouldn't have to worry about

much of anything where Thad Price is concerned. Something else tells me to just go with the flow.

"I have a twelve-year-old son, Sheriff. I'm sure he would love seeing the river, too."

"By all means," he says, sounding somewhat relieved at the prospect of a chaperon. "Bring him along. There's plenty of room, plenty of room for everyone."

In for a penny, in for a pound.

"And a father as well, Sheriff. I know it would make Pop's day to ride down the river's back. Is that too much to ask?"

"The more the merrier," he says, beaming. "We could put in one Saturday morning, do a little fishing, a little boat riding. I know an island just round the next bend where we could have a picnic. It's like no place you've ever been."

I retrieve a business card from my coat pocket and scratch my home phone number on the back. Time to close this deal.

"Hang on to this card, Sheriff. Let us know a day or two ahead of time and we'll drive up one Saturday morning. That's my home number on the back. You won't forget now, you won't disappoint us?"

He seems alarmed at the suggestion of a possible memory lapse on his part. As if such a thing could happen.

"Oh, no. No, no, I won't forget," he says. "Never."

He puts my business card in his shirt pocket and buttons the flap.

"Bring along some of your own family, Sheriff, and we'll make it a party. A day on the Mississippi."

"It's Thad," he says. "And there's just me. Just the one."

"Then that would make four of us, Thad?"

"That makes four," he says.

We stand toe to toe atop the levee with our eyes meeting, but speech, for the moment, has become expendable. I feel a tickling itch.

Once the sheriff has tucked his tall frame into the cruiser and headed back down the levee, I take another long look at the Mississippi. Off to my left, I notice a dirt road that leaves the foot of the levee and enters the russet-brown forest beside the shore. Squads of willow and cottonwood trees crowd the low riverbanks fighting for a toehold against the onrushing flood. Through the leafless trees I can see the one-lane, heavily rutted dirt road that runs along the river for several hundred yards before arriving at the edge of an abandoned landfill. The meandering drive will take me through a landscape of thickly wooded swamp and bottomland. Unfit for cultivation or cattle grazing, the terrain looms alien and dense and inhospitable.

A perfect place to stash these empty diesel cans.